HEX AND THE SINGLE WITCH

M.J. CAAN

VINCI BOOKS

By M.J. Caan

Singing Falls Witches

Thank you, as always to B. You make everything possible.

Vinci Books

vinci-books.com

Published by Vinci Books Ltd in 2025

1

A CIP catalogue record for this book is available from the British Library.
Paperback ISBN: 9781036705626
The EU GPSR authorised representative is Logos Europe, 9 rue Nicolas Poussion, 17000 La Rochelle, France contact@logoseurope.eu

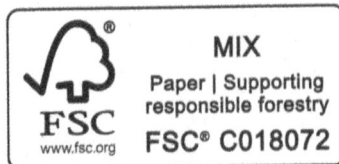

FSC
www.fsc.org

MIX
Paper | Supporting responsible forestry
FSC® C018072

Printed and bound in Great Britain by Clays Ltd, Elcograf S.p.A.

Chapter One

"Are you sure you're okay with this?" Torie questioned. "I mean, it's only a long weekend, but still."

Elric laughed softly and turned over to face her, using one hand to softly push a strand of hair out of her eyes.

"I think I'll be fine," he said. "Besides, you don't need my permission to go on a girls' trip with Jasmin."

Torie frowned. "Is that what it sounded like? That I was asking permission? I wasn't. I just didn't want to say I was doing it as if you had no opinion on the matter."

"Oh? And what if I said no, I didn't want you to go?"

Torie laughed. "Well, you'd get over it."

Elric smiled and rolled over, stretching. "It's fine. Besides, I may have to make a quick trip back up north to help with a council matter. So, I probably won't even be here when you get back."

Torie got up, quickly reaching for her robe and throwing it around her before standing.

"Why do you do that?" Elric asked.

Torie felt heat rise into her cheeks, and she was glad he couldn't see her face.

"How's that going? Establishing a new council to lead a new pack of werewolves made up of two previously warring clans can't be easy," she said. It was clear she was trying to change the subject and she knew it wouldn't work.

"Don't deflect," Elric said. "I find you so beautiful and yet you always seem in a hurry to get dressed."

Torie sighed and turned to face her boyfriend. He had moved to the top of the covers and was sprawled out naked on the bed.

"See, I don't think I will ever be that comfortable in my skin. It must be a wolf thing."

Elric nodded. "You're right. Shifters are more comfortable naked than in clothes. We feel less confined. I just wish you could see yourself the way I do."

Torie sighed and wished that were possible. She knew she still carried baggage with her from her failed marriage. She was aware that it might be baggage she would carry forever, but she was trying.

Her ex-husband had never wanted to see her naked and made it a point of telling her to cover up. He also had been the type to always remind her to not eat so much bread when they were out, and to ask when her next Pilates or aerobics class was. Thinking back on this now, she realized he probably wanted to know where she was at all times so he could plan his sneaking around with another woman behind her back.

Well, that had certainly come back to bite him. He was spending the next twenty-five years to life in a federal prison because of that decision. She knew she should have felt bad for him, but she just couldn't.

She had finally found the strength to forgive him for his

affair, and that was about as good as she could be in the situation. She had spent so long thinking horrible thoughts about him and wishing ill on the man, that she now felt ashamed of herself for putting such things out into the universe. The fact that she had nearly died saving his child and his fae mistress more than balanced the karmic scales as far as she was concerned.

During her trip down memory lane, Elric had moved to the edge of the bed to sit next to her. He placed an arm around her waist, pulling her into him.

For a second, Torie flinched, reflexively reaching for his hand to move it from her side. She could hear her ex's words clearly in her mind the morning he mentioned something about a muffin top and then laughed it off.

But this wasn't him. This was a real man; one who had accepted her and her muffin top and made her feel like she was the most important person in his world.

She leaned over and kissed him.

"Thank you," she said.

"For?"

"Being you. You never cease to amaze me."

He smiled and stretched languidly. "Thank you. But don't change the subject. I know what you need. I have a great idea." His eyes twinkled mischievously.

"And what might that be?" she asked, a slight frown making its way across her features.

"We are having a naked weekend as soon as we are both back from our trips."

Torie had to fight the urge to let her mouth drop open. "I'm sorry. A what?"

"You know. A naked weekend. We are going to spend the entire weekend naked. I'll stock up the fridge and make sure we have everything we need so we don't even have to leave the house."

Torie fought to suppress the laughing fit she felt coming on. The look on her boyfriend's face told her he was absolutely serious, however.

She patted him on the chest as she made her way towards the bathroom. "You hold onto that thought. I'm going to shower and get dressed. Jasmin should be here soon to pick me up. We need to get going; we still need to drop Leo off at Fionna's."

"I feel bad I can't stay here with the little guy," Elric said.

"Don't even worry about it. He gets along great with Fionna, and she is ecstatic about keeping him for a few days."

Finding a dragon sitter wasn't easy, and Torie was thankful that Fionna got along so well with her pet.

She made her way into the bath, careful to shut the door behind her before dropping her towel.

"Hold up. He said what?" Jasmin asked.

She and Torie were in the kitchen, packing some snacks and bottles of water, and a few last-minute road trip items they may need.

Torie looked around making sure Elric wasn't within earshot. Of course, with werewolf hearing, she was pretty sure he could hear them from outside if he wanted to.

"He said he wants to have a naked weekend when I get back," Torie said.

Jasmin roared with laughter. "Girl, that is some wolf nonsense right there. I told you what could happen if you started dating one, but oh no, you had to get your swerve on with a supernatural."

Torie playfully flung a paperback at her friend.

"Keep your voice down! And why aren't you appalled at the idea?"

"What is there to be appalled at? He's not wrong; you are a bit of a prude."

Torie was about to answer when she heard the front door chime. Elric entered the kitchen, smiling at Jasmin.

"Okay, all Torie's stuff is loaded in the back. You two are all set. Although, I have to ask, what's with all the pillows? They don't have those where you're staying?"

"Of course they do," said Jasmin. "But I need *my* pillow. I can't sleep on a different one."

"Same here," said Torie. "It's an age thing."

"Well, I hope you guys have a great time. Don't think about this place at all. For the next few days, Singing Falls and all its craziness is not your concern," he said.

Torie couldn't help but frown a bit. "Well, I mean, everyone does have our number in the event that something happens, right?"

Elric rolled his eyes playfully. "Of course they do. But nothing will happen. And even if it does, Max is more than capable of dealing with things on his own."

Torie let out a deep breath. He was right. The town's resident werewolf sheriff had more than proven himself lately. Still, she had grown to love everyone in this community and couldn't help but worry. Something rubbed against her shin, and she looked down to see Leo pressing his weight against her, his wings shimmering as he pined for her attention.

She patted her shoulder and the little dragon lifted off

the ground and landed on her arm, making his way up to perch on her shoulder, nuzzling into her hair.

"And I'll only be up north with Sable for a bit. Then I'll be back to help keep an eye on things as well," said Elric, reaching forward to scratch under Leo's chin.

"And you'll call if you need something?" Torie questioned.

Before he could answer, Jasmin took her by the hand to drag her out of the kitchen.

"No, he won't call," she said, turning to glance back at Elric. "If anything comes up that you can't handle, well… too bad. Deal with it until we get back. But do not call her."

They were out of the house and piling into Jasmin's sleek new Jaguar drop top when Elric caught up with them. He handed a paper bag to Torie with a smile.

"I picked this up this morning for you. They are the last of the elderberry scones from Jim's. He wanted you to have them."

Torie couldn't help but smile as she opened the bag and inhaled the aroma of the freshly baked scones.

"Oh my. Thank you! That was so thoughtful, Elric."

He shrugged in response. "It was nothing. I knew that with this being the last weekend the bakery will be open, you'd miss them. Although I hear Fionna has almost badgered Jim into giving her the recipe for them."

Torie laughed in response. If anyone could convince the former owner of the bakery to give one of his most prized recipes to the new owner, it would be Fionna.

Torie sighed as she wrapped her arms around Elric. He was right. She needed a break and some down time. Taking over the bakery with Fionna and Jasmin would eat up much of her free time when she returned.

This might be her last chance to get away for some time.

Elric gave her a squeeze and planted a kiss on the top of her forehead. She breathed in his scent and looked up into his eyes.

"I'll see you in a few days," Torie whispered to him.

He nodded before releasing her and opening the car door for her. Bending down, he smiled in Jasmin's direction as she climbed behind the wheel. "Have fun, safe trip."

"Don't worry. I'll take good care of her. I won't let her do anything I wouldn't do myself," Jasmin said, slipping on her sunglasses.

Elric frowned as Torie slipped into her seat.

"That's not very comforting," he said, shutting Torie's door and waving to them as they pulled out.

"Whew, that man has it bad," said Jasmin, giving Torie a playful look.

She didn't say anything but was painfully aware of the hint of red that was no doubt creeping up her neck. She smiled. Elric wasn't the only one who had it bad.

"Is he okay?" asked Jasmin.

"What? Yeah of course. He's just going to miss me."

"No, not the wolf, your dragon," she said, nodding at Leo who had curled into a ball on Torie's lap.

Looking down, Torie could see the little dragon had his eyes closed and was snoring lightly. Tiny wisps of smoke unfurled from his nostrils as he snored lightly. The spiny ridge that ran down his back vibrated, running through a variety of colors from deep reds and oranges to bright greens and pinks.

"Huh. I've never seen him do that," said Torie. "He must sense that we are leaving him for a bit. We really haven't been separated since we got him."

"He's attuned to your emotions. So, I'm betting he is more worked up than usual because you are."

Torie pursed her lips and glanced at her friend. "Point taken. I really am looking forward to this. And thank you for suggesting it."

"Oh, you aren't the only one who needed a getaway. I haven't had a break in some time." She glanced at Leo and then Torie. "I hope he's going to be okay staying with Fionna while you're away."

"They get along great. He'll be just fine."

Chapter Two

He was, in fact, not fine at all.

If anything, Torie developed newfound admiration for Fionna's skill at wrangling an unhappy dragon. Leo cried and threw a tantrum like a toddler being left out of the fun stuff by their older siblings. He clung desperately to Torie, wailing incessantly, as Fionna tried to peel him off her.

Finally, she was able to lure him to her side with a slab of uncooked ribeye steak; that had Leo licking his tiny, sharp teeth; eyes wide in gluttony as he followed her back into her house. Torie and Jasmin waved to her as they backed out quickly before Leo could change his mind. Torie found herself hoping the little guy was all huff and puff and didn't burn Fionna's house down.

"Well, that was fun," Jasmin said.

"It just goes to show that I should socialize him more. Maybe spend time around other people with him before he gets…" She trailed off, not wanting to think about what she was going to do with a fully grown dragon as a pet.

"Before he gets big enough to eat someone?" Jasmin finished.

"Well, I wasn't thinking about it like that, but thank you for putting that image in my head."

"Next time we will go somewhere dragon friendly, so he can come along as well. And we will bring Fionna also. It feels weird not having her along."

Torie nodded. Even though they both knew Fionna needed to spend some time with her wife, Glen, it was tough not having her bubbly self tagging along for the ride.

"Well, I think we should establish some ground rules," Jasmin said.

"Such as?"

"Well, no talk about boyfriends. Or relationships. Or—"

Torie held up a hand to cut her off. "Wait, why do I feel like that is aimed solely at me?"

"Well, if the wolf fits...," said Jasmin. "And honestly, you know I love you, and you know I am...starting...to love Elric. But this weekend is about us relaxing and living life. Not him."

Torie didn't say anything as she pondered the rule.

"And you're not going to be able to do that, are you?" said Jasmin.

Torie laughed. "Well, how about if I promise to try my best?"

"Good enough."

"Then I have a rule as well," Torie quipped.

"Go for it."

"We can't just automatically say no to something just because it is outside of our comfort zone."

Jasmin offered her a sly glance. "Oh, you must be talking about you. Cos I know you're not trying to throw a jab at me."

Torie laughed. "Okay, Miss put-any-sauces-on-the-side-cos-I-don't-want-any-of-my-food-touching-any-of-my-other-food."

Jasmin pursed her lips and focused on the road ahead.

"Don't blame me because I like to enjoy the taste of my food without it being contaminated by the flavors of everything else on the plate," she replied.

They both laughed and then rode in silence for a bit before Torie spoke up.

"So, what is this place we are going to again? Where did you hear about it?"

"It's called Greenview Resort. It's supposed to be one of the best in the country. Five-star experience all the way around. Great food, spa...oh and naturally heated underground mineral baths. I can't wait. We are in for a long weekend of pampering."

Torie looked at the navigational screen in the center of the console that was leading them on their grand adventure.

"I've never been to West Virginia," she said. "Not even on a layover flight to anywhere."

"Well, it's not really on the way to anything. If you're going to West Virginia, it is the final destination."

"This is where you grew up, right?" Torie asked.

"The state, yes. But not where we are going. I grew up in the poor, mining communities in the southern part. Most of them are just ghost towns now, so there is nothing to go back to. But the central portion, where we are going, was always like some mythical Hollywood to me as a child; a place you always heard about but would never have the means to visit. So, when I heard about this world-renowned spa that opened there, I figured it would be the perfect getaway for us."

"Well, it looks like we are going to pass through a lot of

attractions on the way there. We can stop for some sight-seeing along the way."

Jasmin frowned, glancing at the clock.

"Maybe. But I don't want us getting there too late. It would be nice to walk the grounds some before it's dark."

Torie fiddled with the navigation system a bit more, scrolling through the list of interesting places to see, before clearing her throat and turning to Jasmin.

"You know, there is something I really think we need to talk about."

"Does it have to do with your pet...the dragon or the wolf?" She turned and flashed Torie a smile. "Sorry. Couldn't resist."

"Haha. No, it has nothing to do with either of them. It has to do with us."

"Oh? In that case, I'm listening."

"I've been thinking about what we found out... about us."

Torie could see the tension rise in Jasmin as she readjusted her hands on the steering wheel, gripping it slightly harder.

"And I can't figure out if what we were told was the truth or some elaborate lie," she continued.

"Well, I say look at the source it came from. That old shapeshifter was lying to us. It wanted to get into our heads and throw our game off."

"That's what I thought," said Torie. "But then, I wondered what they would get out of lying to us about that. But also, my mother adored you. Why would she do that if we were from two different, and warring, covens? Why would she have introduced us? And your mother never said anything about covens that shouldn't interact, right?"

Jasmin shook her head. "But my mother died well

before my magic kicked in. We never got to have any of those mother-daughter bonding moments."

Torie fidgeted with her seatbelt momentarily. "I went to the town hall to see what I could find out about our families."

Jasmin turned to face her briefly before returning her eyes to the road. "And?"

"Well, my old surname—Deadman—definitely wasn't one of the more popular names in the county. They were known for their secrecy and generally not the nicest family to get along with. I traced your name back as far as I could find it, but there is no hint of it in the records after a couple of generations."

"Probably because I didn't grow up here. As far as I know, I have no family in the region. We were all from West Virginia."

"That's what I was thinking. And I mean…well, since we are going to be in the state…" Torie let her voice trail off.

Jasmin let out a hard laugh that almost sounded more like a bark. "No way. I haven't been anywhere near my hometown in ages. Even if we made that drive, I can assure you there is nothing there that will be of any use to us. That place was dying when I left; I'm betting there isn't even a town hall anymore."

"But it wouldn't hurt to check. Plus, it's literally on the way to the resort," Torie said. "And just think, you can show me all the old places you used to play as a kid. Where you went to school, where you—"

"Okay, okay, I'll think about it. Maybe we can look at leaving the resort a little early and drive down there before heading back home."

Torie didn't say anything as she shrank back into the plush leather seat and stared out her window.

"Fine. But that means we have plenty of time to stop along the way for food." She rummaged around finding the paper bag Elric had presented her with. "Oh, we can have scones now."

"Uh-uh, missy. You put that back. You are not eating those greasy things in my car. That will be a snack when we pull over for gas."

Torie smiled as she pretended to pout. Something told her this was going to be a great little adventure they were headed on.

"There, now isn't this nicer than sitting in a gas station parking lot?" Torie said.

They were just over three hours into their road trip, and she had convinced Jasmin to take a forty-five-minute detour to an overlook along a mountain pass. The scenic beauty that spread out before them was unrivaled. The overlook was situated above a valley pass between two mountains, with the valley and meandering river flowing magically beneath them.

They sat on a picnic table enjoying their scones, as well as a basket of cheeses and cucumber sandwiches that Torie had made. The fresh, crisp, mountain air bit at their cheeks as the sun started its downward arch for the evening.

"I have to admit, this is breathtaking," said Jasmin. "I'm not sure it's a match for our mountain, but it's certainly up there." She stood up, stretched, and began gathering their things. "C'mon. We've lost time. If we don't make any more stops, we should get there just before the end of the day."

"Why are we in a hurry? What's so important about being there before sunset?" Torie asked.

"Well, if we're there before it gets dark, we can walk the grounds and see if we need to set up any protection wards."

Torie stopped just as she was packing the plates back into the picnic basket.

"Jasmin, why would we need wards? We are on vacation, remember?"

"Yes, we are on vacation, but we are not going to be stupid. There is mess everywhere, and you know it. Better we are prepared than caught off guard."

Torie stood there, her hands on her hips as she stared at her friend.

"Jas, this resort has been around for a few years now. It's populated by normal, everyday humans, having a perfectly normal time. I don't think we are going to need protection wards." She went back to packing the basket and then was struck by an idea. "Hey, what if we add another rule to our trip. A no-magics rule."

Jasmin looked at her, blinking her eyes almost comically before she started walking around slowly, looking down at the earth and scraping the toe of her shoe through the dust and grass.

"What are you looking for?" Torie asked.

"The rock you must have fell on and bumped your head," came the reply.

Torie couldn't help but laugh. "C'mon, I'm serious. We are trying to get out of Singing Falls for a couple of days. So, it should be physically *and* mentally. We leave the magic behind us for a few days. Besides, we don't want to attract attention."

"We are hex witches, Torie. We are going to attract

attention wherever we go. It just might not always be the humankind."

That was something Torie had been wondering about, and she made a mental note to ask Jasmin about it later, after their road trip. Had Singing Falls always been such a bizarre hot spot for supernatural activity gone wrong? Or had it all started after Torie had to move to town? And if so, why?

"Again, all we are agreeing to do is try our best to stick to a rule. This one doesn't have to be hard and fast either; but let's at least try."

Jasmin rolled her eyes but smiled and nodded. "Okay. But I'm telling you right now, if we get jumped by some hell demon and killed, I promise you my last words will be, 'I told you this was a stupid rule'."

Torie couldn't help but laugh as she finished packing up the basket. They dropped the trash in the nearby receptacle and climbed into the car.

"Okay, if we head back to the highway, we can just make it before sunset," Jasmin said, firing up the engine.

"Or," said Torie as she punched at the navigation screen. "We could take this road that winds through the mountains and enjoy the views." She pulled up an alternate route and pointed at the screen.

Jasmin frowned looking over the display. "It will definitely be dark once we arrive if we go that way."

"But we don't have wards to worry about now. Besides, I want to see the countryside."

Jasmin sighed, knowing she wasn't going to win this one. "Fine. But we better not get lost. It gets cold at night up here this time of year."

Torie nodded and settled back into the seat. She knew that her friend wasn't just giving in. She was enjoying the trip as well, and, just maybe, she was starting to relax a little.

With a sigh, Jasmin eased the Jaguar onto the road, turning away from the highway and towards the more scenic backroads that would take them to their destination.

One hour into the detour, and a half-hour after passing the last gas station in sight, the check engine light came on, followed by a lot of flashing lights on the dash, followed by the car locking up and crawling to a stop on the side of the deserted road.

Chapter Three

Torie deliberately avoided eye contact as they popped the hood and got out of the car. She took the lead on looking around at the engine, most of which was concealed by a large cover, and wiggling a few wires.

"So, what exactly is wrong with it?" Jasmin asked, folding her arms over her chest.

"Um, I'm not a mechanic, but I don't see anything wrong."

"But you were just touching everything like you knew what you were doing."

"Well, nothing came loose, and the engine isn't hot. Or it doesn't feel hot, so I guess it didn't overheat," Torie replied.

"Why would it just suddenly overheat? Do cars suffer from spontaneous combustion? And before you answer, that was rhetorical."

Torie didn't speak as they looked at one another for a moment then back at the car.

"Okay, you can say it," she said.

"Say what? That we should have stuck to the main highway where there would be cars whizzing by every few seconds? No. I'm not the type to say something like that."

Torie took a deep breath. "Well, someone likes their sarcasm laid on with a snow shovel."

Jasmin sighed in reply. "Okay. Let's just figure out what our next move should be. It's going to be dark soon."

Torie rested one hand on her chin as she fell deep into thought. "Well, there was that cut off we passed back there that said something about a hotel. We could start walking."

"In the dark? No way. What if there are bears?"

"Bears, Jasmin? Really?"

"Okay, well maybe there are bear shifters. We're not in Singing Falls anymore. Who knows what could be running around the wilds of West Virginia. We *are* in West Virginia, aren't we?"

Torie nodded. "Yes, we passed the state line marker a few miles back. And we are witches. We've faced a lot worse than bear shifters. Besides, isn't this your old stomping ground?"

"Not this part of West Virginia. I have no idea where we are," said Jasmin. She took out her phone and held it up. "No service. Do you have any?"

Torie mimicked Jasmin's movements, holding her phone high as she walked around the car. "No. None here either."

"Well, we could wait here by the car. Surely someone will come by," said Jasmin.

"Or we could walk back towards town and flag down someone. Or maybe we'll at least get phone service."

Begrudgingly, Jasmin agreed, and the two set out walking in the direction they had just come.

"I just don't get what happened with the car," Jasmin

said. "It's in perfect condition. I just had it serviced before we left, and there was plenty of gas in the tank."

"Well, think of it like this. We are having an adventure. Maybe this is where we are meant to be."

"I'm meant to be having a pedicure and a champagne facial. Not trudging through the tick-infested back roads of West Virginia."

Torie was about to argue and point out the natural beauty of everything around them when her phone pinged. She looked down and saw two bars showing.

"Oh wow, two bars. Not much but let's see if we can call for assistance. But first, we need to find out where we are."

She opened her navigation program and swiped at her screen a couple of times.

"According to this, we are near a town called Pikes Peak. That sounds nice!" she said. "And it looks like there is a hotel called Valley Plantation. Since it's getting dark, we could stay overnight there if we have to."

She pulled up a picture of a large, antebellum-style house and showed it to Jasmin.

"Uh-uh. That sounds and looks like a place slaves built. I'm not staying there."

Torie looked at the picture again. "You're right. Good point." She swiped the screen a couple more time and then placed the phone to her ear. "But with service, I can at least call roadside assistance."

Jasmin watched as she quickly spoke into the phone while nodding her head, before closing the call.

"Alright, they are sending a mechanic with a tow truck in case he can't get us going. They said to wait by the car. Should be here within the hour."

Together, they turned and headed back for the car, arriving just as the tow truck pulled in behind them.

"Wow, that was fast," said Jasmin.

She waved to the driver and they both watched as he climbed down from the big rig. He was not a small man; he was well over six and a half feet tall, and if the way he filled out his gray tee shirt was any indication, working out must have been his second job.

The side of the truck was painted with the logo, "Pine's Automotive" and a phone number. The large man walked up to the women, waving and offering them a grin of perfectly even, perfectly white teeth. He extended a hand the size of a catcher's mitt and swallowed Jasmin's whole in its grip.

"Hey there," he said, "I'm Trevor Pine. You ladies need a hand?" He then turned to Torie, extending his hand to her in greeting.

"Hello, Trevor," she said. "It's nice to meet you, and thank you for responding so quickly."

"What do you mean?" Trevor said. "I was just on my way back from dropping off Ms. Gorman's car for her and happened across you ladies."

"Oh, so you're not from roadside assistance?" asked Jasmin, casting a quick glance at Torie. "We just called them, and they said they were sending someone out."

"Yep, that would be about all they can do," said Trevor. "Well, that and tow your truck about two towns over and then bill you a truckload of money for it. Good thing I came by when I did."

He walked to his truck and reached into the back to remove his toolbox before heading back towards the two women.

"Let's see what we got here," he said. "Can one of you pop the hood?"

Both women got back into the car, and Jasmin hit the

latch freeing the hood. Once it was up and Trevor had leaned into the vehicle, she whispered quickly, "Torie, he's not with roadside. Who knows who this man could be? He could be some hillbilly killer for all we know. One that drives around looking for random women to prey on."

Torie chanced a glance out the front window to make sure the man was still in view and under the hood.

"Do you think? Well, what should we do?"

"I say we thank him for stopping and then tell him we will wait on roadside assistance. If he tries anything funny, I'm blasting him all the way back to hicksville."

"Hicksville? I thought you said you didn't know this area. Is that where he's from?" Torie asked.

"Girl, I don't know! That was a figure of speech—"

Before she could finish her sentence, a meaty hand knocked on the driver window, making them both jump.

Trevor beckoned for them to step out as he wiped oil from his hands with an already greasy rag.

"Well, good news and bad news, ladies," he said.

Torie and Jasmin looked at one another with worry.

"What is it?" asked Jasmin.

"Your alternator is shot, and I'm pretty sure your electrical system is fried. Did you buy this car used, ma'am?"

"Used? Not at all," said Jasmin. "I've only had it a few months."

"Well, all I can say is it's a Jaguar. They are prone to problems like you wouldn't believe. This one needs some new parts before it's going to run again."

Jasmin let out a long sigh.

"Um, can you fix it?" asked Torie.

Jasmin shot her a look. "Or we could just wait on roadside assistance. I mean, that's a service we pay for…"

"I have a feeling we should go this route," Torie replied. "A gut feeling."

"Sure. I can fix it, but I'll need to order the parts," Trevor replied, his tone a little confused at the back and forth between them.

"So where is the good news in all this?" Jasmin questioned.

"The good news is that I happen to know for a fact that the Henry's have an unexpected vacancy at The Sweetbriar. A couple of their guests cancelled last minute, so you'll have a place to stay in town while your car gets fixed."

Torie gave a nervous glance to Jasmin.

"Oh, we weren't planning to stay overnight," said Torie. "We're actually on our way to the Greenview resort for a getaway, and I'm sure they are going to be expecting us."

Trevor let out a small whistle. "Whew. The Greenview? That's supposed to be the second-best resort in the Virginias. That's a good place."

"Second best?" asked Jasmin. "If that is second best, what sits in first place?"

"Why The Sweetbriar, of course. It's not as well-known as the Greenview, but it's hands-down, head and shoulders above. It's a place that many of the Hollywood stars come and stay at while they are filming movies around here. And you're lucky there is a vacancy. They are hosting this family reunion for some really rich city dweller types from Chicago this weekend, so it will be a hopping place."

"Well, as awesome as that sounds, we really were looking forward to Greenview Resort. How long will it take to fix the car?" said Jasmin.

"Oh, that won't take long. Maybe a couple hours. Three at the most I'd say."

"That's not bad," said Torie. "Could we make it to the Greenview by tomorrow midday?"

"Nope, not at all," Trevor said.

"Wait, you just said it wouldn't take long to fix," said Jasmin.

"It won't. Once the parts come in. That will take a couple days at least. And with it being the weekend, they might not come in until Wednesday, next week."

Torie and Jasmin just stared at the man and then one another.

Trevor seemed to sense the uneasy tension that passed between the women and raised a finger. "You know, there is a train in the next town over that can take you up to the Greenview. It will be running tomorrow afternoon. I can take you over to it, and you can be in Greenview by tomorrow night if you want. Leave your car and your number at my garage, and I'll call you when it's ready. But that's really the best we can do. You'll have to spend tonight at The Sweetbriar, however."

Jasmin took a deep breath and looked at Torie. "What do you think?'

"It's not like we have much of a choice," she replied. Mentally, she wanted to remind Jasmin about the hillbilly axe-murderer thing but couldn't do it without Trevor noticing.

Just then, the roar of another truck caught their attention as a second tow truck eased up behind Trevor's. Another man, a little older and nursing what looked like a bad knee, walked up to them, tipping his baseball cap at the women. He gave Trevor a once over and barely grunted in his direction.

"What's the problem here, ladies?" he said.

"Are you from roadside assistance?" Jasmin asked. "We

have some car trouble and…well, this gentleman happened along and was helping us out."

"Uh huh," said the second man, glancing past Trevor at the Jaguar. "Fancy ride you got there. We can get you fixed up."

"Oh? Do you need to know what the problem with it is? Trevor here says that the—"

The tow truck operator raised a hand. "Honey, I'm sure whatever it is, the garage over in Tinsel can handle it. They know fancy."

Torie was taken a little aback by his demeanor but decided to let that pass since, technically, he was there because they had called for him.

"How far is Tinsel?" she asked.

"It's a couple towns over. I'll be happy to give you and your car a lift there and they can get you fixed up right away. Guaranteed."

"But it needs parts," said Jasmin.

"Maybe it does, but without a certified mechanic to check it, you don't know that for sure. Just hop on in and don't worry your pretty little head about it. I'll take care of everything."

Torie arched an eyebrow as she felt the air around Jasmin began to crackle.

"Rules," she said quickly to her friend as she stepped between her and the driver.

"What rules?" said the man.

"Oh, nothing," said Torie. "You know, I hate that we had you drive all the way out here for nothing, but Mr. Pine has been so helpful, and we have decided to take him up on his offer to tow us into town and put us up for the night at The Sweetbriar."

She glanced at Jasmin who was only just beginning to simmer down.

"Suit yourself," said the man as he turned and hobbled his way back towards the truck. "You have fun staying at The Sweetbriar. Hope you make it the night." He climbed into his truck and cranked the engine, backing away from them slowly before turning across the two-lane stretch of road to drive away.

"What did he mean by that?" Jasmin turned to Trevor.

"Oh, nothing. Just old chatter. People are always saying The Sweetbriar is haunted, but we're pretty sure that's just talk started by the owners to drum up business. No one really believes in ghosts, right?"

Jasmin turned to Torie, giving her a look that would have stopped the other tow truck dead in its tracks.

"Here, let me get all your stuff into the back of my truck. Then I'll have you hooked up in no time and you can be at The Sweetbriar in time for dinner."

They watched as the nice man loaded his vehicle with their belongings, and before long they were pressed into the front seat with him, headed for an establishment that may or may not be haunted.

Chapter Four

When Trevor eased his truck onto the main street of the tiny town of Whistle Lake, both Torie and Jasmin were enchanted by its small-town charm and character.

"This looks like something out of a Hallmark Christmas movie," said Torie, eyes roaming both sides of the street, admiring the bakery, coffee shops, and mom and pop retail stores that lined the cobblestone streets.

They moved slowly past the storefronts until Trevor took a right at the end of the street and proceeded to a less trafficked area that then led to a combination gas shop and automotive repair shop. There were a variety of older cars and trucks parked behind it, next to a large, open car wash station.

"I always return the cars I work on cleaner than they were when I pulled them in," he said, noticing the women looking at the station. "Of course, that won't be a problem with your car. It's a beauty as is."

They waited in the car while Trevor unhooked the

Jaguar and went into his shop to make some notes and check what parts he did have on site.

"Well, he's definitely not an axe-murderer and this place is astonishing," said Torie.

"Yeah, well so is Singing Falls and lest we forget there are plenty of horrors around that sleepy little hamlet," Jasmin replied. "Maybe we cast one simple revelation spell…just to make sure there is nothing hiding in plain sight around here."

Torie turned to her quickly. "Nope. Not even that. We are going to experience this little town like every other normal human being. I can't wait to see what The Sweetbriar is like!"

Trevor returned and climbed into the driver's seat.

"I was right. The parts should arrive on Tuesday. Your car will be ready around midday. I'll take you over to The Sweetbriar now. It's not far and they have bikes you can use if you want to make a quick run over to Main Street in the morning."

"Oh, I can't tell you the last time I was on a bike," said Jasmin. "Just the thought of it makes my knees hurt."

Trevor looked over at her and smiled. "You look like you're in fine shape to me. I bet you could show any bike who's boss."

Jasmin shushed him with a slight giggle and playfully swatted at his arm. Torie looked over, quickly raising and lowering her eyebrows comically at her best friend.

"Trevor, since it seems like we will be here at least for tonight, what would you say we need to do or see?" Torie asked.

"Well, definitely have the breakfast at The Sweetbriar. Penny, she's one of the owners, will put out a spread of delicious homemade biscuits, country ham and gravy, eggs, apple butter, made from apples grown on the property, that you will have to taste to believe.

"But then, if you can manage it, try and visit some of the stores here on main street. One-of-a-kind gifts that you can't get at the big online retailers. And of course, there are the hot mud baths that will work magic for your joints."

"Magic, huh?" said Jasmin, sneaking Torie a glance. "That might be worth checking out."

"Oh, I don't know," said Torie. "Sounds like an awful lot to try cramming into a morning."

Jasmin ignored the remark as they made their way through some winding back roads before turning onto a large, U-shaped driveway, the middle of which was in front of one of the most beautiful stone homes either of them had ever seen.

It was a revival-style home, with intricate stonework complementing the two plus stories and the beautiful slate roof. Ivy covered much of the front, creeping above the windows and framing the pronounced, majestic center of the home. Massive chimneys jutted upward from points at either end of the home as well as points in the center. There were three wide, slate steps that led to the front porch, which was complete with a swinging seat suspended from the covered ceiling, and multiple rocking chairs arranged for the guests to oversee the perfectly manicured front lawn.

"This is amazing," said Torie.

"If you think the front is nice, wait until you see the back. There are two terraces on ground level and one on the second that overlook the grounds and the sunset," said Trevor as he climbed out of the truck and moved to the passenger side to open the door. "Just bring your purses; don't worry about your bags. I'll be sure they get to your rooms. Let's get you checked in first."

They made their way down the flagstone path that led to the porch. There, Trevor opened the large, black iron and glass door and held it for the two ladies.

Inside the entryway was a large, circular table that contained a stunning, polished stone vase filled to overflowing with an immense flower arrangement. There were flyers neatly arranged in front of the flowers that listed various local attractions and restaurants to visit. Behind the table was an imposing, grand staircase that led to the second floor.

Trevor led them to a room on the right-hand side of the entry, where they were greeted by a smiling woman well into her sixties.

"Penny, I'd like you to meet Torie and Jasmin," said Trevor. "They had some car trouble just outside town and it won't be ready for a few days. I knew you had that cancellation this weekend, so I was thinking…"

"Say no more," said Penny. "The Baxters had to cancel on account of the little one getting sick. They had a connecting suite, and I would be happy to put the two of you in it. And since it's the only one left, I'll even charge you the rate for two doubles instead of the suite rate. Seems only fair."

"Oh, well, thank you, but that doesn't seem fair. I mean, technically you're doing us the favor by putting us up," said Torie. "Let us pay—"

"I just will not hear of it," said Penny with a dismissive wave of her hand. "You will not pay that rate. The rest of the bed and breakfast is pretty full, so we are not going to quibble over pricing. Got it?"

Something about the finality of Penny's words told them there was no changing her mind once she had made a decree like that, so they just smiled and nodded.

"I'll get the bags," said Trevor, turning to leave the room.

Penny rang a small bell that sat on the checkout counter. "Kitty will be out to help you bring them in." She looked up at the two women and offered a smile. "Kitty is our housekeeper. She helps with all the tasks around the inn. If you need anything at all and you can't find me or Brad, just look for Kitty; she can help you. Oh, and Brad is my husband. You'll meet him soon enough."

Torie perused the room, looking at the scenic area shots and old pictures of the inn. One black and white photo in particular caught her eye, and she pointed it out.

"Who is this?" she asked. The photo showed three people standing in front of what was clearly The Sweetbriar, but many years in the past. There was a man and a woman, along with a child. They didn't smile but stared straight ahead into the camera, their weatherworn skin a testament to the hard, physical labor that was expected of everyone at that time.

"Oh, that's my husband's parents and Kitty's mom when she was a child. Kitty's family has been a part of ours for so many years now."

They finished checking in, providing their email address and their billing information before Penny turned her back, picked out a couple of keys from a peg board behind her, and then led them out of the reception area.

"You'll be on the second floor, near the terrace," Penny said. "Your suites have the best views, and you also have a private, Juliette balcony off each one. In the morning, complimentary coffee and Danishes will be delivered to your suite, though I suggest you come down for the breakfast. It's included, and I personally cook everything you'll be eating."

"Yes, we've heard about your apple butter so we can't wait to try it," said Torie.

Penny offered a heartfelt laugh, clasping her hand to her chest. "That has to be Trevor talking. I swear that boy can eat his weight in food and not gain an ounce." She shook her head in delight as she gave them their keys. "C'mon. I'll show you to your rooms and then leave you to explore. There's no part of The Sweetbriar that is off limits, so feel free to wander to your hearts' content."

The two women followed her through the beautifully appointed house and up the curving staircase to the second-floor landing. Black iron and glass sconces that mirrored the look of the windows seen from the outside, lined the hallways as they walked to the back of the house. Penny showed them the adjoining rooms, each identical, and the door between them that would allow each to access the other's room if so desired.

The rooms were very spacious, with furniture that struck the right balance between old-world charm and modern comfort. There was a small kitchenette in each and a bath that was everything anyone could ask for.

"Now that looks inviting," said Torie, eying the large, marble soaking tub that sat opposite a walk-in shower. "That will be the perfect place to relax after the day we've had."

"Might I suggest you ring Kitty and ask her to bring you a bottle of peach wine while you soak?" said Penny. "It's a match made in heaven. And the wine is made from locally sourced peaches. Really, everything you experience here is locally sourced, from the food to the bedding and furniture. All crafted here in the low country from local artisans."

"Impressive," said Jasmin. "But what is this I hear about your hot mud baths?"

"Oh, now that is something special indeed. We can show you where those are in the morning if you like. But they aren't open at night; the area around them can be tricky to maneuver in the dark."

"Sounds wonderful," said Torie. "What about these ghosts that we heard about? Is this place really haunted?"

Jasmin shot her friend a look that said, 'You just couldn't help yourself'.

Penny chuckled at the question. "Oh, darling, that is just part of the charm of this place. You can't have a house this old, with the kind of storied history that The Sweetbriar has, and not have a chain-rattler or two. But I will say this; any spirits walking these halls are about as benevolent as they come. So don't you be worried about that."

She placed the keys in their hands and turned to leave, just as another woman entered the rooms, with Trevor following close behind.

"Kitty," said Penny. "I'd like you to meet our new guests. They will be joining us for the night...maybe a little longer if they have a good stay."

Kitty smiled and nodded at the women, dropping a couple of bags, and Trevor did the same, placing the ones he carried next to those that Kitty dropped.

"Where would you like these?" Kitty asked.

She appeared to be in her late forties, was on the shorter side and seemed stout of build. Her dark hair was pulled back in a bun that mimicked that of Penny's, and the gray shirt and matching pants were cut to fit her frame perfectly. Looking at the woman, Torie's mind was taken back to the old photo downstairs. Kitty was the spitting image of her mother.

"Oh, don't worry about that," Torie said. "We can take them from here." She reached into her purse to take out some money and offered it to Kitty, who politely smiled and waved her off.

"Thank you, but no. Tipping is not expected here," she said.

Reluctantly, Torie returned the bills to her purse, not wanting to make a scene.

"Well," said Penny, "we will leave you two to get settled in. There is a door at the end of the hall to the right that leads out onto the terrace if you're interested in getting some fresh air before bed. And again, feel free to look around. If you need anything at any point in your stay, just pick up the phone in your room and press zero. Either myself, Kitty or my cantankerous husband will pick up."

"Ladies," Trevor said, nodding as he backed out of the room. "I'll call you with updates on the car."

Once they were alone, Torie and Jasmin moved their individual bags to their rooms and then made their way out onto the terrace. True to the description, the terrace overlooked the grounds that stretched from the house to a light undergrowth of shrubs and small dogwoods, before the deeper woods began, obscuring any farther view. There were multiple path entrances at various points along the wooded barrier, each posted with a bright yellow sign that they couldn't make out from where they stood.

"Those must mark hiking trails," said Torie.

"Or all the attractions Trevor kept mentioning. The mud baths, mineral pools and fruit orchards."

The cool, evening air carried the scent of fresh-cut grass, roses, and blossoming fruit all mingled together in a magnificent floral arrangement that delighted the senses.

"It's pretty nice here," said Torie. "And we haven't even seen all that this place has to offer."

"I know what you're getting at," replied Jasmin.

"We can always go to Greenview Resort another time. These people seem so nice and welcoming. Why don't we just stay here for the trip. Besides, I just get the feeling this is where we are meant to be right now."

"It is strangely relaxing here. So, I'm fine with staying. Let's take a walk around this place. Maybe we'll run into one of their Caspers. See if it's really a friendly ghost."

They laughed easily and headed out of the terrace and down the stairs to the main floor of the inn. Making their way into the large kitchen, they were greeted with an array of pastries and fresh breads, as well as jams and jellies on the large kitchen island. Kitty was inside, putting away grocery items from a cloth satchel into one of the two industrial-sized refrigerators.

"Oh, hello," she said. She eyed the island and nodded. "Sorry, that's all that's left, but I have prepared a special late dinner for the two of you. It will be served out on the main terrace in just a bit. Penny was concerned that you arrived just after dinner, so she wanted to make sure you had plenty to eat before bed. You can make your way to the terrace just through there —" she jutted her chin in the direction from which they had come, "—and you'll see where I have one of the tables set up for you."

Even though she was starving, Torie started to protest when they were interrupted by another woman who sailed into the kitchen. She was tall, with the kind of body that hit the Pilates studio hard on a regular basis, and then burned off even more calories by power walking to all her destinations. Her blonde hair flowed freely about her face as if it had a life of its own.

Torie instantly recognized the type of woman she was. She had known plenty like her in her previous life in New

York. This was a woman who was used to having things her way and had no understanding of the word no.

She felt the cold come off the woman as she breezed past her and Jasmin and approached Kitty, her very expensive heels clicking menacingly across the floor.

"Hi, I stated that I would like my evening Oolong tea to be served at the optimal temperature of one-hundred-eighty-five degrees. That is not the temperature it is at. How do you expect me to enjoy it?"

Kitty looked at the woman and then quickly averted her eyes. "I am sorry, Mrs. Perry. You were not in your suite at the time you originally said you would be, so I left it—"

The ice queen held up her hand, stopping Kitty mid-sentence. "If I was not in my suite then you should not have left it. It has been ruined now."

"I will make another and bring it up to you immediately."

"Don't bother. This is not the appointed time I said I would have my tea. I shall simply do without tonight. But I expect everything to be ready for me in the morning for my appointment."

"I will personally see to it that all is in readiness for your spa, ma'am."

"Well, that hardly fills me with confidence in the experience," the woman replied out of the corner of her mouth. "Honestly, I don't know what more I expected from a grown woman with a child's name…"

With that, she turned and strode out of the kitchen, not bothering to grace Torie and Jasmin with a look.

"Kitty, are you okay? That was so uncalled for," Jasmin said, walking over to the visibly shaken younger woman.

"I'll be fine. That's just Samantha Perry. She's one of the guests from Chicago this weekend. She and her husband, plus some of their extended family, are staying at the inn for a reunion of some kind. They are all…used to getting their way I think."

"Well, it doesn't matter who she is or where she's from, that is not okay," Torie added.

"Please, don't let it bother you. But you might want to stay out of their way. I just keep reminding myself they'll be gone in a few days, and we can all breathe a little easier. But please, don't let that ruin your evening. Go on out to the terrace. I'll be out with your meals. There are cards on the table that you can mark your cocktail choices on if you'd like one, and those will be served with the meal."

Torie could see the woman was embarrassed and didn't press the matter any further. Instead, she and Jasmin made their way onto the terrace where they were greeted with an outdoor table for two under a canopy of garden lights.

Walking out to the table, they were caught off guard by a couple of voices speaking in rapid, hushed tones. Huddled in the corner, silhouetted by the terrace lighting, was the unmistakable figure of Samantha Perry, pressed closely against another figure draped in shadows.

At the appearance of Jasmin and Torie, the two quickly broke apart, silently separating as Samantha hurriedly made her way towards the far side of the terrace and a door leading into the inn. The man she had been with sank further into the shadows before disappearing in the opposite direction.

"Oh," said Jasmin, "looks like we interrupted some juicy drama."

Torie frowned. "It sounded like they were arguing."

"Maybe he didn't fluff her pillows the way she liked. Either way, that's not our business. Let's have a nice dinner and a couple cocktails before hitting the sheets. I've a feeling tomorrow is going to be a long day."

Torie nodded as she sat down. She looked at the area where the two figures had been standing and where the male had disappeared into the shadows. There was no exit off the terrace she could see, and no entrance into the building from that side. So where had he gone?

She shivered as a thought raced through her mind.

It was like he was a ghost and had simply vanished.

Chapter Five

The following morning, Torie awoke before Jasmin and went out onto her small balcony to greet the day. The morning air was chilly as she took in a deep lungful of clean air, enjoying the feel of the first rays of sunshine peeking over the horizon. A smell of fresh coffee and baking bread wafted up to her from below, making her stomach growl. She shouldn't be hungry; the small dinner they had late last night had turned out to be a feast. Lamb chops with a fresh mint jelly accompanied by roasted baby potatoes and honey glazed carrots had proceeded a fresh raspberry torte that melted in their mouths. All accompanied by peach-brandy cocktails that packed a serious punch. They had eaten way too much.

Yet here she stood, all but salivating over the thought of more delicious foods just waiting for her in the large, self-service, dining room below. She thought about waking Jasmin but decided to let her sleep in. Maybe she would just go down for a cup of coffee while she waited for her friend to wake up. And if that cup of coffee came with a just-out-of-the-oven biscuit smothered in apple butter…well, who was she to refuse?

After getting dressed, she made her way down to the dining room where a large buffet table was set with plates, saucers, bowls, cups for coffee or tea, and various utensils. She poured herself a cup of coffee from the silver carafe that was sitting out and made her way over to the self-serve food station. Her nose had been correct. There were warm flaky biscuits, honey butter and apple butter, as well as a few different kinds of fruit preserves.

She helped herself to a spoonful of apple butter to go with her bread and made her way out onto the terrace, cup and saucer in hand. Making her way to one of the tables, she sat down her food and looked around the large patio. She assumed she was the only person up at this hour and had the place to herself.

"I probably shouldn't, but…" she whispered to herself before setting down her coffee and making her way over to the spot where she and Jasmin had seen Samantha Perry and the mystery figure last night.

She looked around and saw the direction Samantha had hurried off to, but where had the mystery fella gone? Even though it was ground level, the terrace was bordered by beautifully carved stone railings, connected by iron bars. The man could have jumped over the railing and made his way across the grounds, but surely they would have seen that; even in the uneven light created by the overhead tea lights strung over the terrace.

She walked back to the corner of the terrace where it connected to the building and saw something she hadn't noticed before; a tall but narrow door built into the side of the house. There was an iron handle that jutted out, and she found herself drawn to it; one hand inches from grasping it when she was startled by someone clearing their throat behind her.

She spun around to face an older man dressed in loose-fitting, faded jeans and a flannel work-shirt that was only half tucked in.

"Can I help you?" he asked. He carried a large bucket that he sat on the terrace between them.

"Hello, I'm sorry, I was just looking around. My name is Torie. I'm one of the guests here. I was just having a bite of breakfast when I saw this door. I was just wondering where it went."

The man huffed, giving her a slight frown.

"It's an old servants' entrance to the catacombs under the property. That's how they used to bring in food from the farm fields to the house without disturbing the owners. It stays locked now because it's dangerous down there and the lights that were strung along the paths are all out and haven't been replaced."

"Interesting," said Torie, eying the door. "Is it always locked?"

"As long as I've been here, and that's a pretty long time."

A thought flashed through Torie's mind as she made the connection. "Are you Mr. Henry, Penny's husband?"

"Yes, ma'am, that would be me. I was just about to take these beets into the kitchen to have them cleaned and prepared for lunch today." He indicated the bucket at his feet before looking back to Torie. "You and your friend are the ones with the car trouble Penny was telling me about last night."

She nodded and extended her hand in greeting. "Yes, that would be me. Thank you for your incredible hospitality.

This inn is amazing. I have never seen anything quite like it before."

"Well, that would be all Penny's doing. She has worked years to make this what it is. She tells me what to do and I do it; that's been the secret to our success with this place and our marriage."

Torie chuckled, taking a liking to the old man instantly. She was about to say something when she saw his face gather like a darkening sky before a storm and his eyes glinted hard at something over her shoulder.

She turned and saw a man stepping out onto the terrace. He was short, with reddish hair combed straight back that undoubtedly tried to hide a bald spot. He wore small-framed glasses that somehow made his round face seem puffier than it probably was as he scanned the terrace, hands on his hips. He saw Mr. Henry and locked eyes for a moment, before turning his head unceremoniously and making his way back inside.

"Who is that?" Torie asked.

"Ah, just one of them uppity guests in from out of town. Whole family of them have descended on The Sweetbriar for a reunion. Not the nicest of people, but then, I guess if I had spent all my days figuring out how to screw everyone I met out of money, I'd be pretty ornery too."

She was tempted to mention the interaction she witnessed last night between Samantha and Kitty but decided it wasn't the time for that. Kitty seemed capable of handling the situation, and she didn't want to risk making her uncomfortable around her employer.

"Well, thank you for your time, Mr. Henry," she said. "I just wanted to say how lovely your home is."

"Please, call me Brad. And I hope you enjoy the rest of your stay." He nodded, picked up his bucket, and headed towards a door on the side of the terrace that undoubtedly led straight into the kitchen.

Walking back to the table, she was met by Jasmin, carrying a cup of coffee.

"Thought I'd find you out here," she said. "You should have woken me."

"Uh, you were snoring up a storm. Sounded like you needed the rest."

Jasmin's eyebrows arched. "I don't snore. I don't know what you were hearing but it was not snoring."

Torie opened her mouth to speak, but Jasmin cut her off. "End of story."

Smiling, Torie changed the subject. "Did you try these biscuits? They are heaven!"

"Ugh. Maybe later. the thought of more food is not sitting well with me. However, I did just see Penny, and she said no one will be using the hot mineral springs today, so if we want to go, we will have them to ourselves. I figured we could wander into town and then take advantage of the springs later. What do you think?"

"I think that sounds perfect. Oh, and I just met Brad. Mr. Henry. He's so nice. I found a door over there where Samantha was huddled up last night! He said it leads to a catacomb network that is no longer used. The door is locked, but I'm thinking that is the only way the second person could have gone last night when he disappeared."

Jasmin leveled a look at her. "Why are you obsessing over that? I'll bet you anything whoever was with that woman was not her husband. So, you know what that means, right?"

"Yes, that she is probably having an affair."

"No. That means whatever she is doing is not our business."

"But don't you think it's odd the way he just disappeared? And that door is locked, so where did he go?"

Jasmin shook her head. "Nope. Not odd because I don't care. Now finish up the biscuit, go get changed, and meet me at the bikes. We are heading into town."

The ride into town, while fairly short, was every bit as painful as Torie had expected it to be. She had been negligent on going to the gym lately, and it showed. She hadn't brought her knee brace, because the trip was supposed to be a luxury resort where the most stringent activity would have been deciding what her next cocktail would be. There was nothing physical planned so therefore, no need for a brace.

Now she wished she had it. Her knees ached and she was sure her back wouldn't be thanking her the next day. Still, despite all of that, she was so happy to have made their trip into town. The foliage they rode through was breathtaking, and as it was still early, there was not a lot of traffic to worry about.

They pulled their bikes up onto the sidewalk where Main Street began and looked around.

"I just realized, the inn didn't give us any chains to lock this with," said Torie.

Jasmin looked around and shrugged. "I'm betting this place is like Mayberry. No one will take them."

Together, they started down the cobblestone sidewalk, stopping to peer into shop windows along the way. Some were just starting to open, and the proprietors would wave or step out of their doorway to introduce themselves and tell them to stop in anytime. Everyone they met was warm and welcoming and only served to reinforce the idea that they made the right decision by staying in town while the car was being fixed.

They stopped at a window with the words "Whistle Brew Creamery—Coffee and Dessert Bar" painted across it. They exchanged looks and a mischievous smile and darted inside.

Immediately, they were hit with the delicious aroma of fresh coffee beans and baked goods. The store was on the quaint side, with a single counter taking up the far wall ahead of them, and a couple of bar-height, small tables arranged in the picture window with no chairs. The wall behind the counter was painted with chalkboard paint and the daily specials were scrawled across it in neat penmanship.

No sooner had they approached the counter than the double doors at one end of the shop swung open and a man in his early forties, tall, dark-skinned, wearing silver-framed glasses and an orange tee shirt with the coffee shop's logo emblazoned on it, stepped into view. He flashed them a smile that caused his face to light up and nodded in their direction.

"Hello and welcome to the Whistle Brew. What can I get you?"

Torie stole a glance at Jasmin and saw that her friend was immediately smitten with the man before them.

"Um, um...I guess I'll have some...a..." Jasmin stammered.

"We will both have a cup of your passion tea to go," said Torie, butting in and giving Jasmin a fun poke in her back to haul her back to the land of the living.

"Yes. Passion. That's what we want," blurted Jasmin. "Tea! Passion tea, that is."

The man nodded, turned his back to them, and began

working at the dispensary tap, emptying the fluid into two paper cups.

Jasmin turned to face Torie, eyes wide as she struggled to hold back a smile. She silently mouthed the words "Oh my God". Torie looked back at the man helping them, her face freezing in sudden panic.

Jasmin followed Torie's eyes and saw a large mirror mounted above the chalkboard wall. In the reflection of the man's face, his eyes twinkled as he watched the two women.

Torie immediately felt her face turn red as he spun around to face them, drinks in hand.

"I don't recognize you ladies. Are you new to town?"

"We're just visiting," managed Jasmin. "Staying at The Sweetbriar and thought we would come check out Main Street."

"Excellent decision," he said. "My name is Cameron. Cameron Leeds. Welcome to my little shop on Main."

"You're beautiful," said Jasmin. "Your shop is beautiful, I mean."

"Thank you," said Torie, hoping to rescue her friend yet again. "My name is Torie, and this is Jasmin. How much do we owe you?"

"Oh, it's on the house. You're my first customers of the day. Consider this a welcome gesture. I'll let you pay when you come back." He hit them both with another dazzling smile.

"So, Cameron," said Jasmin, "is there anything in particular here in town that we should make it a point to see? Other than this fine establishment I mean."

"Hmm," he said, scratching at his chin. "I would say the bookshop a couple doors down. Lots of rare first editions in there. Oh, and Jamie's Candy Shop across the street. If you have a sweet tooth, she has some confections that will blow your mind. And I guess, if you're into it, the crystal shop at the very end of the street. Emily, the owner, can tell your fortune."

"Oh, really?" said Torie.

"Well, like I said, if you're into that. She has quite the following though. Lots of people believe in her. I mean, I think it's all just the power of suggestion myself. But she thinks she's a witch or something, so just take what she says with a grain of salt."

"A witch, huh?" said Jasmin. "Now that might just be something to look into."

Chapter Six

"Now, how could we possibly not stop in there?" said Jasmin.

The two of them stood outside a large picture window that looked into the last shop at the very end of Main Street. Because it was at the end of the building row, it had more space and considerably more light pouring in as there were windows on three sides.

Unlike other shops, there was no painting of the name on the window. Instead, there was a sign hanging from the roofline above the front door.

"The Witching Well," said Torie. "Catchy."

They walked into the shop and were greeted by the scent of burning incense mixed with lavender. The store was filled with large bookcases and freestanding displays that managed to tame the large space and make it feel cozy. There were tables set up in the middle of the shop with various knick-knacks for sale, and beyond those was a long counter with a glass top displaying items that could only be accessed from the opposite side marked "Employees Only".

They stood at the display, gazing down on crystals in various shapes and colors. There were also a few perfectly round, black stones that looked like marbles sprinkled throughout the crystals as well. Something about them drew Torie's attention and she couldn't stop staring.

"Hello, can I help you?" came a chipper voice from behind the ladies.

Torie started, turning to find a woman in her mid-forties, with bright green eyes and tightly curled hair that she kept cut short.

"I'm Emily Belmont. Is there something you'd like to see?" she asked.

"Hello there. I'm Torie and this is my friend Jasmin. We were just admiring Main Street and saw your shop and thought we'd step in." She held out her hand in greeting, but the woman just looked at it and smiled, nodding.

"Well, it's nice to meet you. Welcome to The Witching Well."

Her hands remained at her side, and Torie saw that she wore small, tightly fitted, green gloves made from a delicate woven fabric.

Torie motioned to the display. "Those black stones. What are they? May I see one?"

"Those are Hypersthene stones. Very rare. They are for grounding oneself during deep meditation and they assist in opening the third eye; allowing one to see that which is hidden from them," Emily said.

"May I see one?" Torie asked.

Emily hesitated for a moment, glancing from Torie to the stone and back again, before walking around the counter to where the sliding door accessing the trays of crystals could be opened. She reached in and withdrew one stone, handing it over to Torie.

"It's...amazing," said Torie as she examined the piece. "Are there bits of color inside it?"

"Sometimes, there can be flashes of blue or gold inside, depending on the spirit of the person holding it."

"This is so beautiful. Jasmin, look at this. Do you see the colors?"

Torie held it out for her friend, who peered at the stone.

"Looks black to me," Jasmin said with a shrug.

"How much is it?" said Torie.

"Those are three hundred," said Emily.

Jasmin coughed, nearly choking on her words. "Three hundred what? Dollars?"

"As I said, they are very rare," Emily replied with a smile.

"I'll take it," said Torie, fishing out her credit card.

Emily smiled and took the card, heading for her cash register.

"Are you crazy?" demanded Jasmin in a hushed whisper. "Three hundred dollars for a marble?"

"There is something about it. It...called to me," said Torie.

Jasmin stared at her friend but didn't say anything. She just nodded and moved to look around the store.

"Here you go," said Emily, returning with Torie's credit card and a small, velvet bag for her to place the stone in. "Keep it in this bag at all times, except for when you are holding it in your hand. From this point on, it belongs to you; don't give it over to anyone else." She sent a quick glance in Jasmin's direction before returning her gaze to Torie.

She accompanied Torie over to the wall of books that Jasmin was looking through. They were the typical fare of spell books for beginners, love spells for the forlorn, good luck spells to make you rich; all the type of charlatan works that could be found in any dime store magic shop across the country.

"Something tells me you aren't really interested in any of those," said Emily. "But I have something over here that might interest you."

She walked over to the back of the shop and took a box off one of the shelves, placing it on a table in front of the ladies. Lifting the lid, she revealed a black book with intricate, gold runes inlaid across the cover.

"What is it?" asked Jasmin, frowning.

"It's a one-of-a-kind spell book, written in a dead language," Emily said.

Unable to help herself, Jasmin opened the cover of the book slowly, looking at the words etched on the yellowing paper.

"Can you read it?" asked Emily.

"What? Of course not. It looks like Sanskrit or something," said Jasmin, before closing the book and looking away.

Emily was watching her with curious eyes that caught Torie's attention.

"What is it?" asked Torie.

"Well, that book is blank. There is nothing written on the pages; at least nothing that appears to my eyes. Or anyone else's I've ever met. But you saw writing," said Emily.

Jasmin narrowed her eyes. "Probably just a trick of the light."

Emily stared at her for a moment. "Yes. Probably." She led them away from the table before offering up another, wry smile. "So, how are the two of you enjoying your stay at The Sweetbriar?"

"How did you know that's where we are staying?" asked Jasmin.

"Well, she just paid three hundred dollars for a rare stone without batting an eye. I'm betting the two of you came into town in that Jaguar that Trevor towed into his garage. That tells me you are both people of means. Which means you're probably staying at The Sweetbriar, since it's the swankiest place around."

"Well, you're right. That is where we are staying. Everyone here has been so nice and welcoming," said Jasmin.

"Uh huh," said Emily. "Well, just be careful. That place is haunted. And not necessarily by ghosts."

Torie frowned. "What do you mean?"

Before anything else could be said, a bell attached to the front door chimed as more guests filed into the shop.

"Excuse me," said Emily. "I need to help some regulars." She walked towards her guests, before stopping and turning back to Torie. "Remember what I said about that stone."

They left the shop and made their way back down Main Street, admiring all the gift shops that were starting to fill up with more people as the morning stretched on.

"Well, hey there, Ms. Torie, Ms. Jasmin," came a voice from behind them.

They turned to see Trevor's beaming face. He was dressed in a blue uniform and carried a mailbag.

"Trevor," said Torie. "How are you? And please, it's just Torie and Jasmin."

He smiled and nodded at them. "I'm doing great. How are you? How are you finding your accommodations?"

"Everything could not be better," said Jasmin. "It's as

incredible as you claimed it was. But what are you doing dressed like a mail carrier?"

"Oh, that's because I am the postmaster in town. At least until another one can be found. Mister Jeeves, the original postmaster, up and had a heart attack on us. I worked there part time with him, so they gave me the job until someone else can be found."

"I'm so sorry," said Torie. "When did that happen?"

"Oh, about four years ago now," said Trevor.

"I'm sorry, did you say four years?" asked Jasmin, a confused look on her face.

"Yes, ma'am," he replied. "But don't worry. Cars still come first. I do mail runs first thing in the morning before anyone is up and then mind the cars after that. So yours will still be up and running when I said it would."

Torie could only smile at the look on her friend's face. "Hey, Trevor, you must know everything about everyone around here, right? Being the mailman for so long I mean."

"Pretty much," he replied.

"Well, do you happen to know anything about the coffee shop owner, Cameron? Specifically, is he single?" Torie asked.

"Cameron Leeds? Why no, he isn't single. He's been married for as long as I can remember. He and Mike Drake have a place out on Taylor's ridge. Beautiful home. You should ask for a tour someday."

"Ah figures," said Jasmin, under her breath.

"What was that?" Trevor asked.

"Oh…nothing," Jasmin replied with a smile. "Just saying that he makes a great cup of tea."

"Oh, he sure does," said Trevor. "Well, I guess I better get going. Still a couple more packages in here to deliver." He patted the satchel slung obliquely across his body.

"Nice seeing you, Trevor," said Torie. "And one last thing. What about Emily Belmont? We were just in her store, and she helped me pick out the most perfect gift. If I wanted to send her a thank you, what would be the best way to see that she gets it?"

Trevor paused, pursing his lips. His eyes darted back and forth a couple of times before he leaned in close.

"I'd say it would be best if you just dropped it by her shop in person. She doesn't like anyone coming to her house. So, if you want her to get something, you need to get it to her." His face took on a serious tone as he nodded again. "Ladies."

They watched in silence as he quickly headed down the sidewalk in front of them without looking back.

"Do you think that was odd?" asked Torie.

Jasmin shrugged. "Maybe she conned him out of three hundred dollars too, so now he's like, get your own mail."

"Did you sense anything coming from her? Anything magical?"

"I wasn't feeling for that. No magic use, remember?"

Torie didn't say anything as they continued walking back towards their bikes. They walked slowly past the coffee shop, gazing surreptitiously through the window at Cameron as he served hot coffee and blazing smiles to his customers.

"I don't know who this Mike fella is, but dang is he a lucky one," Jasmin said. She took one last wistful look, and they continued on until they reached their bikes.

Torie looked at hers with disdain. "Is it too late to call a rideshare? We could put the bikes in the back."

Jasmin laughed. "Just think how amazing those hot springs will feel after a workout like this."

The trip back to The Sweetbriar was quicker and easier

for them, and by the time they arrived, Torie was almost sad the ride was over. They walked into the inn and were greeted by a cacophony of raised voices and people talking over one another.

Torie and Jasmin sidled up to Kitty, who stood outside the reception room watching as multiple people were talking at the Henrys at once.

"What in the world is going on?" enquired Jasmin.

Kitty took a deep breath. "It appears that Samantha Perry has gone missing. Her husband said she never came back to their room last night after going out for a walk."

Chapter Seven

Torie grasped at Jasmin's elbow, pulling her aside.

"Oh no! What if we were the last ones to see her last night? What if that other man had something to do with her disappearance?" she said.

"Calm down. We don't know what, if anything, has happened to her. I mean, what if she was having an affair or something and ran off with someone else? Look at the way these people are carrying on; I wouldn't blame her for wanting out of this family."

"Yes, but don't forget, she was just as awful as they seem. What if something bad happened to her?"

Jasmin crooked her head and looked back at the scene unfolding.

"I'm sure she's fine. Maybe she had a fight with her husband and is just blowing off steam somewhere. I mean, we don't even know who her husband is."

"It's that gentleman there," said Kitty. She had obviously been eavesdropping on their conversation as she pointed out the same man Torie had seen earlier in the morning on the terrace.

"I saw him outside this morning," she said to Jasmin. "He gave Mr. Henry a nasty look and then went back inside."

"Don't worry. You weren't the only ones to see her outside last night," said Kitty. "The town sheriff is on his way over to take statements."

"You really shouldn't be listening in on other people's conversations," said Jasmin. "It's not considered polite."

Kitty looked nervous, glancing around the room. "I'm sorry. You're right. It's just that all of this has me so upset. They're going to question me the most."

"Why would you say that?" asked Torie.

"I'm the help. I'm always the one who gets questioned if anything happens."

Instantly, Torie's heart went out to the girl, yet all she could offer was a sympathetic smile in support.

"Who are all those people?" she asked.

"Samantha's extended family. The husband, Walter, there," Kitty said, pointing, "his brother Jacob, and his wife Millie, standing off by herself."

Torie's eyes followed Kitty's finger around the room. The two men were doing all the yelling at poor Brad and Penny, who looked beside themselves as they attempted to calm the brothers.

"Are they the only ones staying here? Doesn't seem like much of a reunion," said Jasmin.

"Yes, it's just the four of them. They were able to book up most of the rooms so that they don't have to be on top of one another. Apparently, the two brothers haven't spoken in years, and this is more of a business reunion than a personal one. They own some kind of business together and have all agreed to meet to handle some big sale coming up," said Kitty.

"Wow," said Jasmin. "You really do hear everything that goes on, huh?"

Kitty blushed and looked away. "When you're the maid, most people tend to forget you're in the room."

There wasn't much either of them could say to that, so instead, Torie and Jasmin excused themselves and headed upstairs to their rooms.

"Let's freshen up, meet back downstairs in one hour so we can head to the springs," said Jasmin.

"You still want to do that?"

"Of course. I'm betting this whole thing will be sorted out by then. Samantha will show up in time for her afternoon Oolong or whatever she has them create, and all will be right in Richie Rich's world. You'll see."

An hour later and they were dressed in loose-fitting, comfortable sweat suits that covered their one pieces, with extra towels in hand as they prepared to depart for the mineral springs in the wooded area to the back of the inn's property.

"There, that's them," came a voice from behind as they were on their way out the back terrace door.

Turning, Torie saw Penny heading their way, waving one hand. Beside her a tall mustached man in a policeman's uniform strode along beside her.

"Torie, Jasmin," said Penny as they approached, "this is Sheriff Benjamin Odette. He's questioning everyone who was at the inn last night. You ladies are the last two."

"Hello, Sheriff Odette," said Torie, offering her hand.

"Please, call me Ben," he said.

"How can we help you, Ben?"

"I'm looking into one of the guests who has gone missing, and I'm asking everyone who was here last night when was the last time they saw her." He took out a small, flip notepad and opened it. He had a tiny pencil in his shirt pocket which he withdrew and licked the lead end. "So, did you know the missing woman, a Ms. Samantha Perry?"

"Know her? No," said Jasmin. "But we saw her a couple of times."

"When was that?" the sheriff asked.

"Well, we saw her just after we checked in. She was speaking to Kitty in the kitchen in an extremely rude manner," said Jasmin.

"Then we saw her again last night, late, probably close to ten. She was on the lower terrace speaking to someone, but we couldn't tell who," added Torie.

"Was it a man or woman she was speaking with?" asked the sheriff.

"It was a man. But it was dark in the area of the terrace where they were standing so I couldn't get a look at him for a description."

"Could you make out what was being said?"

Torie shook her head. "I'm sorry. It really was just a brief glimpse, so there isn't much I can say."

The big sheriff looked them both up and down and scribbled something in his notepad. "You aren't from around here, are you?"

Jasmin returned his look, tilting her head slightly to one side. "Does that matter? Are the Perrys from around here?"

"Depends on who you ask," he replied.

Torie started to ask a clarifying question but thought better of it. "Sheriff, do you need anything else from us? We were just on our way out."

"No, no, that's all I needed. For now. If you think of anything else, here's my number." He handed Torie a card with the town's police emblem printed on it, along with his name and contact information. "But, maybe, don't leave until this is all settled." He then tipped his hat at the two ladies and turned to walk away.

"I'll show you out, Sheriff," said Penny.

Once they were out of earshot, Jasmin turned to Torie. "Don't leave? What was that about?"

"Did you notice the way he said it depends on who you ask, as to whether or not the Perrys are from this area?"

"And?"

"I don't know. But it sounded ominous," Torie replied.

"Girl, everything sounds ominous to you. Are you ready to go find these hot water springs and relax?"

Together, they exited the back of the inn and made their way across the terrace to the steps leading down to the expansive backyard. Once they crossed the lawn, they could make out the signs that marked the trails leading into the woods.

There was one printed on wood that had been painted blue. It read "Thermal Springs and Spa" with a black arrow pointing into the woods.

They walked for about five minutes before coming to an area that had a large, sunken, natural pool surrounded by banks of rock and undergrowth. The water was a murky color with wisps of steam wafting off the surface.

"It smells like peppermint," said Torie. "How is that possible?"

"I think it smells amazing. I've been looking forward to this ever since we got off those bikes."

She took off her sweats and laid them on the rocks at the entrance to the pool, then carefully dipped one toe into the water.

"Oh, this is very warm," she said, easing her way into

the pool. She waded across to the far side and sat down on one of the built-in seats, sinking into the water up to her neck. "Come on in, this is amazing."

Torie followed suit, leaving her sweats next to Jasmin's as she made her way across the pond to sit next to her.

"It's so relaxing," she said. "It feels like there are micro bubbles scrubbing away at me."

She leaned her head back and closed her eyes, luxuriating in the feel.

"What in the...?" she said, opening her eyes. "Are there fish in this pool?"

"What are you talking about?" asked Jasmin, opening her eyes.

"I swear something just brushed against my leg. Oh! There it is again."

She reached down, feeling around where she was sitting. Jasmin watched as Torie's eyebrows furrowed, and then grew wide.

"What is it?" asked Jasmin.

A horrified look crossed Torie's face as she raised her arm, and in her hand, she held a forearm. She pulled the arm up and screamed as she realized it was attached to a body. One that rolled over onto the top of the water when she kept tugging.

Immediately the women recognized the face of Samantha Perry. Leaping out of the pool, they stood in shock staring at the woman who was now bobbing up and down in the mineral-enriched water.

Behind them, from deep within the woods, came a snapping of branches that caused both women to whirl about, trying to discern where the noise came from.

"Um, about that no magic rule," said Jasmin.

"Yeah, that's off the table."

As one, their magic flared to life, flowing through their bodies and down their arms to form glowing circles around their clenched fists. There was more snapping of branches in the forest, and tentatively, they headed into the denser growth.

The overhead foliage choked off more sunlight, and they found themselves moving through shaded areas, pushing branches out of their way as they got closer to the source of the disturbance. Just ahead, there was a low voice, mumbling something they couldn't understand.

Jasmin looked at Torie and nodded. As one, they burst through the final bit of shrubbery, using their magic to clear a path for them.

There was a man with his back to them, looking upward into one of the large pine trees with binoculars. He spun around in surprise, falling backwards into the tree and landing on his backside. Torie unleashed a blast of light meant to disorient the man, causing him to throw his arms in front of his face, shielding his eyes.

Before he could recover, the two witches were on him. They stood over him, Jasmin placing one foot on his chest to keep him pinned to the ground.

"Who are you and what are you doing creeping around here?" she demanded.

The man seemed stunned and blinked rapidly, trying to get his sight to focus through the brilliant pops of light that danced in his periphery. Torie silenced her power, nodding for Jasmin to do the same.

"What? Who are you, what was that?" queried the man, looking from one to the other in confusion.

"We asked you first," said Jasmin.

He started to move and both women stepped back quickly, raising their hands in front of them. Not sure what to expect, the man stopped moving, then held his hands up.

"I'm just going to stand up. That's all," he said with a grunt as he struggled to rise. Once he was standing, he slowly lowered his hands to his side, and Torie and Jasmin did the same.

"Who are you?" demanded Torie.

"My name is Mark Bevel," he said, rubbing a hand over the back of his head.

"And why are you sneaking around the woods here, Mark Bevel?" asked Jasmin.

"Sneaking? I'm not sneaking. I'm tracking an American Bittern," he replied.

"Is that code for married, rich women?" Jasmin said to Torie.

"Huh?" replied Mark. "I don't know what that is supposed to mean, but I work for the Wildlife Survey and Conservative, the WSC. There has been a sighting of a very rare bird that has made its home here in this area. I'm trying to prove that these are its nesting grounds so the land can't be sold to developers."

"So, you didn't just kill a lady and dump her body in the mineral pool back there?" questioned Torie.

He looked at the two of them as if they had each just grown a second head. Then, holding one hand up to show that he meant no harm, he slowly reached into his jacket pocket and pulled out a badge.

"Ma'am, I am a lawfully licensed government employee. I'm not here to hurt anyone, I promise you." He returned the badge to his pocket, still moving just as slowly. "Mind telling me what you're talking about?"

Torie motioned for him to follow them back through the forest. She explained that they were staying at the resort on the property and were trying to have a relaxing evening in the natural hot springs when they discovered a body.

They led him back to the mineral pool where the body of Samantha Perry was still floating in the steaming waters.

"Oh jeez," he said, one hand on his mouth. "That's Mrs. Perry."

"You know her?" asked Jasmin.

He nodded. "Unfortunately, our paths have crossed. Her family is the one trying to buy up this piece of land so they can knock down that fancy resort and develop it into a strip mall. They want to bring the city out here to the country; and they've made plenty of enemies in the process."

Chapter Eight

Jasmin and Torie sat together under one of the grove trees, just outside of the cordoned-off police area around the pool. It wasn't like on television where the area was swarming with CSI techs and tons of detectives interviewing everyone. No. There was only the sheriff and two of his deputies as they stood around waiting for the coroner from the next town over to show up and take the body away.

The sheriff had taken their statement, complete with casting them suspicious eyes, and also interviewed the environmental agent as well.

"So, you've been out here from sun up to sun down for a couple of days now looking for a bird? And you didn't see or hear anything suspicious?" asked the sheriff.

"Nothing at all. But when I'm working, I'm pretty much lost in nature. I have recording equipment with me that I play back at intervals to see if I can hear the delicate call of the American Bittern. I didn't even hear these two ladies until they came out of the woods and scared the daylights out of me." Mark pointed in Torie and Jasmin's direction, to which they responded with a smile and a nod.

Sheriff Odette nodded in return before turning back to the Wildlife worker.

"Funny thing, Mark; I didn't know you were in town," said the sheriff.

Mark frowned. "Well, as you know, wildlife conservation does not fall under your jurisdiction, Sheriff Odette. I'm a government employee and given discretion to move into areas as deemed necessary."

The sheriff nodded and waved a hand. "Oh I know all that. I mean, typically, the Fish and Game authorities notify the senior officer in an area when one of their agencies is active in said area. I got no heads up about anyone working this property."

Mark shrugged his big shoulders. "Maybe they haven't been able to get around to notifying you just yet. The agencies are very short-staffed right now; everyone is running around doing two jobs it seems."

Sheriff Odette looked at the field agent, pursing his lips. "Yeah. You're probably right. One last thing. I know all of you environmental agents wear tracking beacons. If I needed to verify that you weren't actually at the pond, I could do that, right?"

"Absolutely. My field director back at the agency can give you my whereabouts down to within two feet of accuracy."

Ben nodded and thanked him before moving off, heading for the two witches who had been watching the exchange with interest.

"Here he comes," said Jasmin. "Stick to the story."

"What story? We literally climbed into a hot spring and a body popped up. End of story," replied Torie.

"So, ladies, help me out here. The two of you just happen to be out enjoying one of the many hot springs here on The Sweetbriar's property, and it happens to be the one with the body of a missing guest in it, right?" said the sheriff.

"Yes," said Torie, firmly. "That is exactly what happened."

"Are you suggesting something else?" said Jasmin, looking him in the eye.

"I'm saying you were the last people to see the victim alive, and then you happen to be the ones who stumble across the body."

"We weren't the last two," said Torie. "What about the man we told you she was talking to?"

"Yes, we looked into the mystery man. There was no one at the inn unaccounted for. We spoke with everyone, but no one was outside with Mrs. Perry," he said.

"No one that will admit to it, you mean," added Torie.

Sheriff Odette didn't say anything, but he did scribble in his notepad. A voice called out to him, and he looked up, waving at an older man in a gray poncho.

"Looks like the coroner has arrived," he said to the ladies. "Excuse me while I go fill him in on what's going on and we try to figure out the best way to get the body out of here."

When he walked away, the two witches turned just as Mark Bevel was approaching. He nodded, one hand holding the back of his neck.

"I take it the sheriff still has no clue what happened?" he said.

"I think he thinks we had something to do with it," said Jasmin.

"Probably not. Ben Odette has been around these parts long enough. He has some kind of idea in the back of his mind about this; he's just not tipping his hand just yet. Until he's ready, he'll make everyone feel like they are a suspect."

"Maybe it was an accident," Jasmin said. "She could have been here alone, relaxing with a bottle of wine or something, and just passed out in the water; accidental drowning."

Torie looked at her out of the corner of her eye. "Yes. that seems plausible."

"Except that woman was a workaholic and a health nut," said Mark. "She only drank tea and water. I don't see her being that careless."

Torie gave him an eye. "You seem to know an awful lot about her."

"Well, I make it my business to know who I need to keep an eye on. This whole area is a nature preserve. Yet somehow, the Perrys have managed to get a ruling reversing that status. I didn't even know that was possible. Next, they are working on putting together bids for the property and figuring out how to force a sale. That's why they are staying at The Sweetbriar. They're intimidating the owners to make them want to sell. They're also getting the townsfolk riled up with all this talk about malls and big box stores."

"I don't see why they need that here," said Torie. "It doesn't seem like it could be supported."

"You'd think," replied Mark. "But that's part of the grand plan. The Perrys see this town as a potential booming location to draw in big spenders. There is so much nature here they want to exploit it with summer resorts, winter skiing, fall leaf peeping, etc. They are going to build tracts of vacation homes and fill it with their rich friends and their money. Without a care as to what it will do to the wildlife."

His voice grew terse, and Torie saw a hardness move into his eyes that she had only rarely seen on the faces of men. It was a look that usually popped up when they thought they were cornered and were going to have to do something they didn't like in order to get free.

"And you're here to do what again?" she asked.

"If I can show that these are the nesting grounds of one of only a handful of American Bitterns remaining, maybe I can approach a national court to declare the property a sanctuary. No developing. Ever."

"And do the Perrys know you are trying to do this?" questioned Jasmin.

"I doubt it. I mean, I'm still standing so I assume they haven't found out yet. That's one of the reasons I'm staying at the Traveler's Motel off route 6. I wanted to keep my presence here secret."

Torie watched as his eyes tracked to the sheriff as he was speaking with the coroner.

"You think the sheriff might let them in on it?" she asked.

Mark didn't say anything, just leveled the sheriff with that same steely gaze.

"If this wasn't an accident—" started Torie.

"It wasn't," said Mark, butting in.

"—Then who would stand to gain the most by killing Samantha Perry?" finished Torie.

The wildlife agent shrugged. "More like who wouldn't. Maybe you should ask some of the town folks what they thought about the Perrys. Heck, ask her brother-in-law what he thought about her."

Both Torie and Jasmin looked at the man, but it was

clear from his demeanor he wasn't saying anything more on that subject.

"Just be careful at The Sweetbriar," he said.

"We know," said Jasmin. "Ghosts."

He gave them both a bewildered look. "I don't know anything about ghosts, but I know there are people at that inn who aren't what they appear. Just watch your back is all I'm saying."

"Thank you, but we can take care of ourselves," said Torie.

"Oh, I'm sure you can. Speaking of, what did you hit me with when you came up on me in the woods? My head is still aching."

The two exchanged mischievous looks.

"That? It was just a new cell phone app for women. Designed to stun a man with a flash of light so we can run away," answered Torie.

"Well, it certainly worked," he said, shaking his head. "I'm sure I'll see you ladies around, but if you need anything, you know where to find me," he said, heading back through the woods, before turning to them one last time. "Just remember what I said. Watch your back."

They watched as he disappeared through the brush before turning to some commotion down by the pool. One of the deputies was showing something to the sheriff and the coroner that they both appeared to be very interested in.

Torie and Jasmin made their way to the spot where they were all standing, their backs to the two women. The sheriff turned and stopped them as they approached, holding up two hands.

"Hey, careful, this is still a crime scene," he said.

"Did you find something?" asked Torie.

Sheriff Odette looked at them but gave no indication if anything of interest had indeed been recovered.

"If we did, I would not be at liberty to say anything," he replied. "For that matter, the two of you really should head on back out of here. I'll come find you if I need to clarify anything in your statements."

They didn't like the sound of that, but nonetheless did what the sheriff asked of them, and made their way back towards the Sweetbriar.

"Well, that was a bust of a day," said Jasmin. "What say we get changed and head into town? Maybe grab a cup of coffee?" She shot Torie a wicked smile, bouncing her eyebrows up and down a couple of times.

"I mean, if I have to," she replied, laughing. "Oh, and it will give us a chance to ask some of the locals about their interactions with the Perrys. Like Mark suggested."

Jasmin frowned. "I don't think we should get involved in this. This is clearly human drama. We shouldn't go meddling."

"Jasmin, a woman is dead. The least we can do is try to help find out what happened to her."

"I don't know. They obviously have a competent sheriff in charge of the investigation. He may not be very likable, but he seems to take his job seriously. Maybe we should do as he says and just stay out of their way."

They walked on in silence for a few minutes before she turned to Torie again.

"We're not going to stay out of their way, are we?"

Torie laughed and hooked her arm through her friend's as they made their way out of the path into the backside of the resort.

As they approached the back door on the terrace, they could hear the anguish coming from inside. Loud voices were arguing but were also drowned out by the wail of a female voice, crying in despair and hurt.

"I'm telling you; we will sue you! You thought things were bad for this dump before, well you just wait until my lawyers are finished with you. Why was she out there alone? There are no safeguards that could have prevented this so-called accident? Well, you're going to beg me to take this place off your hands by the time I'm finished with you!"

It was Walter Perry, Samantha's husband, who had zeroed in on the Henrys and was going in hard on the hapless resort owners.

Torie recognized Walter's brother, Jacob, who was the polar opposite of his shorter brother in looks. He was attempting to console a petite woman crying in his arms.

"Walt, maybe now isn't the time to—" he started.

Walter wheeled on his brother, one finger jutting out in the taller man's direction. "You shut your mouth. I'm betting your attitude would be a little different if it were your wife found bobbing up and down in a mud pit."

The harshness of his words stung Torie and made the woman crying in Jacob's arms wail even louder.

Walter turned, facing the Henrys yet again.

"Sir, I can assure you that we are fully cooperating with the sheriff's investigation. This was a tragic accident, and we cannot imagine how you must be feeling," said Brad as he drew his own wife closer to his side.

"No, you can't imagine what I'm feeling. But rest assured, you will."

With that, he turned and stormed out of the room, nearly knocking Torie down in his haste to get to the stairs.

"Okay, that was uncalled for," said Jasmin. "And that definitely sounded like a threat."

Torie heard her friend's words but barely acknowledged

them. Her eyes were fixed on the brother as he comforted his own wife. There was something vaguely familiar about him; his height, the broadness of his shoulders, the way he leaned in...

Her eyes went wide as she realized where she had seen him before. He was the man on the terrace last night with Samantha.

Chapter Nine

"Are you sure?" asked Jasmin as they walked down Main Street. They had decided to take a ride-share to town rather than risk more bodily pain by getting on the bikes again.

"Well, of course I can't be one hundred percent sure, because I didn't see his face. But every instinct I have tells me that Jacob was the man Samantha was with on that terrace."

"Wouldn't that just be juicy? Maybe she really was having an affair with her husband's brother!"

"That would definitely be cause for murder," said Torie. She was feeling excited that her friend was getting into the idea that whatever was going on was worth investigating further.

Jasmin stopped and put her hand on Torie's arm. "Is it though? I mean, you found out your husband was having an affair and you didn't immediately jump to killing him."

"No, but he was very lucky I didn't have more control over my powers back then. I would have definitely hexed him. Like impotence-for-life kind of hex."

Jasmin roared with laughter.

"Like tiny-member hexing."

"You mean tinier," Jasmin replied with a laugh.

"Hey, we haven't tried this place yet." Torie stopped outside a storefront that advertised organic, handmade pet food. "Maybe I can find something in here that Leo will eat. It's getting expensive buying him red meat all the time."

"Maybe you should be raising him vegetarian," said Jasmin as they entered the store. "Otherwise, we're going to have to figure out a way to warn the neighboring farmers about keeping their livestock inside at night."

Torie knew she was kidding, but there was a ring of truth to the words. In fact, it was something that had been crawling around in the back of her mind.

"Well, hello there," said the proprietor, coming up to greet them. She was a short, young woman, with hair pulled back in a ponytail and large, frameless glasses. "My name is Krissy. Can I help you find something?"

"Hello," said Torie, looking around. "I have a...dog, that is growing fast and all he seems to want to eat is meat. I just don't think that's healthy, but I don't know what to do in order to get him to try something else. Any ideas?"

The young woman thought for a second, then motioned for them to follow her. She led them down an aisle to a large, glass-fronted, cooler that spotlighted plant-based foods.

"The best way to do that is slowly. You can't just swap out their food because that's bad for their digestion and can create all kinds of problems. I would suggest that next time you are feeding your dog, introduce a little of the new food to their normal, just a bit at a time. And every couple of days, increase the amount of the newer food. You might want to also try adding a bit of bone broth or beef broth to the food to give it a familiar scent. Every-thing in this section has all the proteins that a growing puppy needs without the potential dangers of meat byproducts."

"Those are excellent ideas," Torie responded.

"But of course, it all depends on the type of dog you have. Some are more prone to like red meat than others."

"Yeah, he's kind of like…a wolf. But not a real one."

The woman frowned. "Okay, well that's good. Because if he was a wolf, you're stuck with just feeding him red meat. And lots of it."

Jasmin gave Torie a look and a knowing nod.

"Thank you, we'll take this, Torie said, picking out a tube of what looked like giant sausages.

"Excellent choice. I'll check you out up front," the woman said, leading them back to the checkout counter. "Are you just passing through town?"

"We are. We're staying at The Sweetbriar until our car can be fixed," said Jasmin.

The women arched her eyebrows, turning to them. "The Sweetbriar? Where that poor woman was murdered? Terrible situation."

Torie couldn't help the startled look that passed over her.

The woman waved her hand dismissively. "You know word travels fast in small towns. Especially when it involves those loathsome Perrys."

They made it to the checkout counter, and Torie could tell the woman wanted to continue with her gossip.

"What makes them so loathsome?" asked Torie.

"Well, for starters they worship money. They want nothing more than to buy all the shop owners out on Main Street so they can bring in franchises to cater to their wealthy friends they hope to lure into living here. A few of the owners have agreed, but most are holding out."

"And you?" asked Jasmin.

"I'm on the fence. I'm holding out, hoping they will increase their offer. I want to buy land where I can run a shelter to rehab and care for abused animals. But I need money to do that. As much as I love this store, their money would allow me to do it. But I feel guilty taking the money from them, so not sure what I will do."

"How did they make their money?" asked Torie. "Does anyone know?"

The woman looked around before leaning in and dropping her voice an octave; even though there was no one in the store.

"I heard they made it by fronting a drug company back in the day that created opioids. They were the silent partners in the deal and managed to keep all the money they made from it by selling out their own partners. It was quite the mess from what I've heard. So yeah, I just don't know if I want to fund my dream with money like that."

Torie smiled at the woman, letting her know she respected where she was coming from. "I completely understand, and I wish you the best of luck."

They left the store and headed back down the street in the direction of the coffee shop.

"Well, it seems like that is one shady family," said Jasmin. "If this was a murder, any number of people could have done it."

"Not necessarily," said Torie. "It would still need to be someone who had access to The Sweetbriar, and someone Samantha trusted and knew."

"Like someone she was having an affair with."

Torie thought for another moment. "Maybe. But

honestly, it looked more like they were arguing, now that I think about it."

"Still potential motive," said Jasmin.

"Ha. So you're getting into it as well," said Torie with a smirk.

"Not at all. But it's not like there is anything else to do here while we wait for the Jag to be fixed."

They both came to a stop, eying the store in front of them. It was Cameron's coffee shop.

"Well, speaking of nothing better to do," said Torie with a shrug as they made their way inside.

The smell of roasting coffee was enough to start them salivating as they headed for the counter. Cameron nodded and walked over, flashing them his patented gigawatt smile. "How are my two favorite out-of-towners doing? I heard about the mess at The Sweetbriar. Are you okay?"

"Aw, thank you for asking," said Jasmin. "And yes, we are fine. I mean, it was disconcerting. We were the ones to find the body." She screwed her face up as if the memory was enough to cause her physical pain. "I've never seen anything like it."

Torie was tempted to roll her eyes, but she knew if she did it would be so hard, they might get stuck back in her head.

"Yes, it was jarring. We were down at the organic pet food store and the lady there had heard about it as well," said Torie.

"Word spread as soon as the call to Sheriff Odette was made. His receptionist, Frieda, is like the town crier."

"You obviously know about the Perrys," said Torie. "What do you think about them? Any dealings with them?"

Cameron wrinkled his brow at the thought of the family. "They have their agenda, and it clashes with what I think the core values of this town are. Everyone on Main Street has been able to make a living out of doing what they love; by creating a product that everyone else in town loves and supports. If that family has their way, all of that changes. We become corporate America. All the new franchises will put the mom and pops out of business and will raise prices to the point that your average West Virginian won't be able to afford to shop here."

"So, I take it you're not going anywhere?" prompted Jasmin.

Cameron shook his head, crossing his muscular arms in front of him.

"They will have to drag my body out before I sell to them. Although, from what I've heard, with Mrs. Perry out of the picture, it might be harder for them to make this deal."

Torie's ears perked up. "Oh? Why is that?"

"Well, for one thing, she had all the money in the family, plus voting rights to break any stalemates in buying through their company. Second, there is a rumor going around that she has family in this area. Family that she is trying to keep hidden for some reason."

Jasmin let out a low whistle. "Now how does information like this get out?"

"They've made multiple trips here to town lately while trying to buy out the shop owners. Apparently, they argue a lot up at The Sweetbriar. And that place has a lot of ears..." he replied.

"So we've noticed," said Torie.

"Can I get you ladies a coffee or tea?"

Before they could answer, a buzz passed through the patrons of the shop as Torie and Jasmin turned to see a bustling of bodies rushing past the store window.

Concerned, they followed Cameron out onto the sidewalk where he grabbed a passerby.

"Hey, Woodie, what's going on?" he asked.

The man he grabbed turned, his face slightly flushed.

"The sheriff is here! He's arresting Emily! Says she killed that rich woman from The Sweetbriar!" He rushed off, joining the few other people rushing for the end of the street and Emily's crystal store.

Torie and Jasmin followed, arriving at the crystal shop just in time to see the sheriff leading Emily out of her store, hands cuffed behind her, and ushering her into the back of his patrol car.

"Sheriff Odette, what are you doing?" asked Cameron as the folks around him joined in voicing their own concerns.

"Stay out of this, Cameron," he said, making his way to the driver's side. He stopped before getting in, looking at the small crowd of shop owners assembling. "Everyone, go back to work. This matter will be sorted out in due time. Until then, business as usual."

He climbed in, easing the car into gear. As it pulled off, Emily leaned forward, placing her face against the window as she stared at Torie. She quickly mouthed words before turning back around to settle in the car as it sped off, lights flashing.

"What did she just say?" asked Jasmin.

Torie shook her head. "I don't know. It was too fast to—"

But then she paused as she felt a wave wash over her. The air pulsed around her, lapping at her as she closed her eyes. The pulses changed, becoming words that hit her from all directions.

"In my shop, under the cash register…"

"Torie? You okay? Where'd you go for a second there?" It was Jasmin, and she had a gentle grip on her friend's arm.

"I...I'm okay. I just realized what Emily said." She leaned in close to Jasmin. "I think there's something under the cash register she wants us to see."

The two witches looked at one another, and then over at the store front. There was a deputy leaving, pulling the door shut, and sealing it with a strip of yellow crime scene tape.

"Well," said Jasmin. "Maybe there's more to this town than I thought there would be."

Chapter Ten

The ground beneath their feet was almost all gravel, crunching continuously as they tried to tiptoe along the back of the buildings.

"Can you stop walking so loudly?" Jasmin hissed.

"I'm sorry, but maybe you should teach me how to defy gravity so that my enormous weight doesn't disturb the surroundings so much."

"You're not ready for that spell," Jasmin said casually.

Torie stopped in her tracks. "Wait, are you saying that's real? I literally just made that up."

Jasmin continued creeping towards the back door of the shop. "You'd be surprised at what we can do. When we're ready, that is. I mean, all stories are based on some form of truth. Where do you think the stereotypes of us riding broomsticks came from?"

Torie was flabbergasted and didn't know what to say. Her mind was filled with thoughts around the subject, but she took a deep breath and forced herself to focus on the task at hand. They made their way to the back door, which was locked, just as they expected.

Torie reached out, touching the handle, and pushed a bit of her magic into the lock, popping it open.

"Why does it feel like we are always breaking into crime scenes?" she said, easing the door open.

"I think the better question is, why are we so good at it?" Jasmin whispered back.

Once inside, they made their way through the shop to the checkout counter. There was a half-eaten peanut butter and jelly sandwich on a paper plate, alongside a cup of sparkling water. Emily's purse was still sitting on the floor under the counter as well.

"Looks like she was in the middle of lunch when this happened," said Torie. "But why would they take her and leave her purse?"

"They are probably leaving the scene as is until it can be properly processed."

Torie looked at her friend and clucked her tongue. "The town mechanic is also the town postmaster. Do you really think they have a crack CSI team around here?"

"I'm more interested in how she was able to get her message to you. I didn't hear anything from her," Jasmin said.

"I've no idea. It was like a memory of what she said came to me after the fact. It was a very strange feeling."

They made their way to the cash register, and Torie started to reach for it, but Jasmin grabbed her hand, holding it fast.

"Wait," she said, closing her eyes. "Do you feel that?"

"Feel wh—" Torie stopped mid-sentence as she felt something small and almost imperceptible brush against her skin. It felt like she had put her hand through a spiderweb as invisible gossamer threads tickled her skin.

"That feels like a ward. One that's been erected around the cash register," said Jasmin.

Torie extended her hand, moving her fingers to trace the invisible lines she encountered.

"It's not a ward, at least not like the ones we are used to," she said. "It's more like a...concealment spell."

"Now how would a crystal shop owner in the back-woods of West Virginia know about concealment spells?"

Torie closed her eyes.

"Daughters of the earth, to whom none may lie,
show us that which seeks to hide from our eyes."

The air before them shimmered briefly, before gossamer-blue threads appeared in the air. They floated upward and stretched outward, flowing throughout the store.

"These are fixed in space," said Jasmin, staring at the light.

"Meaning?"

"Meaning, that our little friend the shop-owner didn't cast this spell. It's coming from an object of power. Probably something in close proximity," said Jasmin.

She looked around, holding out her hand, moving it back and forth around them.

"And there you are," she said, stooping to pick up a golden-colored crystal that had been placed under the counter. Holding it in her left palm, she placed her right hand over it and muttered a slow incantation. Immediately, the blue threads disappeared, returning the store to its normal ambiance as the light streaming in through the windows played off the various items of silver and crystal on display.

"Now why would Emily have something like that in place?" Torie wondered.

"Didn't she say look under the cash register?" Jasmin moved to the register and felt around it. "Help me tilt it to one side."

Together, they were able to move it enough to sweep the counter underneath.

"Nothing," said Jasmin.

"Wait; I seem to remember something. When she was being taken away, I wasn't hearing actual words that she spoke; more just the meaning of what she was trying to convey. Maybe what I thought was under the register was really, beneath the register."

She got down on her knees and looked up at the bottom of the counter.

"Ah ha," she said, reaching up to grab at something. "Help me up." She reached a hand up for Jasmin to pull her to her feet. Holding out her hand there was a black flash drive, no larger than her thumb. "This was taped under the counter."

She turned the drive over in her hand. There was no writing or marking of any kind on it to hint at what it might contain.

"Can we look at this on our phones?" Torie asked.

Jasmin raised her shoulders. "No idea. But I don't see how, there's nothing to plug into it. We need a computer for this. Don't suppose you packed your laptop, did you?"

Torie shook her head. "No. This was going to be a relaxing weekend, remember? Can we read it with magic?"

Jasmin pursed her lips for a second.

"No. Magic and technology don't play well together. We'd probably end up frying the thing."

"Well, then, I guess we better go find a computer," said Torie. "But something tells me we shouldn't do it at The Sweetbriar. That place has more leaks than a sieve."

They looked at one another and smiled.

"Great minds think alike," Jasmin said as they walked out the back of the shop.

"Well, you ladies are back awfully quick," said Cameron. "I figured you'd both be back at The Sweetbriar by now. Especially since they've caught the murderer and made everyone feel safe again."

There was an edge to his voice, just under the customary southern charm that everyone south of the Mason Dixon line was so practiced at.

"Do you really believe Emily had anything to do with what happened?" asked Torie.

"Of course not. And I'm betting Sheriff Odette doesn't either. I just don't know why he'd do what he just did," Cameron replied.

"Good. Then maybe you can help us with something," said Jasmin.

Torie held out her hand, showing him the flash drive. "Can you help us get into this?"

The coffee shop owner eyed it like he was expecting it to come alive and bite him at any moment.

"What's on it?"

"No idea," Torie said. "But it might be something that can help prove Emily had nothing to do with Samantha Perry's death."

"Okay. Where'd you get it?"

The two women exchanged looks.

"The less you know about that, probably the better for you," Torie said. She leveled him with a look that let the man know he was probably signing on for more than he might expect.

"C'mon into my office. Let me just lock the door and I'll be right in." He ushered them around the counter to a small room, not much bigger than a utility closet, with a tiny desk and file cabinet as the only furniture in the room.

They heard a series of clicks as he closed the shop before joining them in the room.

"Sorry for the tight quarters," he said. "I'm a one-man shop, so not really a big need for excess space."

"Not a problem," said Jasmin, sliding to squeeze into the space between him and the wall. "Just want to make sure I have a good view of the screen."

He smiled. "It's all good. Let's see what you've got there."

He took the drive from Torie and placed it in the port on the computer. A few clicks of his mouse later and the machine whirred to life. The drive opened immediately.

"Hmm. It's not even encrypted," said Cameron. "Not even a password."

"Well, maybe the person who had it didn't think anyone would be able to find it," suggested Torie.

He looked up from the screen. "Well, you two found it."

"Well, we're not just anybody," said Jasmin.

"No, something tells me you aren't," Cameron said, returning to the computer. "Okay, it's open. Looks like the only thing on here are some spreadsheets."

He clicked around a couple of times, opening them for display.

"What kind of spreadsheets are those," asked Jasmin with a frown.

"Beats me," said Cameron. "There are a lot of layers to it. I'm ashamed to say that my Excel skills are not where they should be for a business owner."

"That's not Excel," said Torie. "Those are bank ledgers. It's a record of transfers of assets and money between accounts that go through a third-party fund manager."

Both Jasmin and Cameron looked at her, eyes wide.

"My ex-husband used to use these. It's a way to hide or launder money. I spent a lot of time in my lawyer's office going over ledgers like this. May I?" She pointed to the screen.

Cameron stood up, offering her the chair. Sitting down, she began expanding and closing cells. As she clicked on certain cells, they contained formulas that converted from symbols into numbers.

"These are large payments being made to someone. Someone who is then hiding them in offshore accounts." She studied the accounts a bit more then nodded. "This explains why she didn't have it encrypted. She wanted whoever to find it to know what was on it."

"But can you see who it belongs to?" pressed Jasmin.

Torie nodded. "Yes. She linked it to the originator's account in New York. And from there…" Her voice trailed off as she made a few more clicks. "To the receiver here. It's…" Again she trailed off, this time her eyes growing wide.

"It's what?" asked Cameron.

"It's a record of money being sent to an offshore account held by Ben Odette. And it's from the Perry trust."

No one spoke for several moments as they absorbed what she had just said.

"Wow. So the small-town sheriff is on the take. He's owned by the family of the woman who was found dead, and he arrested the one person who has proof of his misdeeds," said Jasmin. "I did not see that one coming."

"I can't believe it," said Cameron. "None of this makes any sense."

"Agreed," said Torie. "But if we want to help Emily and find out who really killed Samantha, it needs to start making sense. Is there anyone else in the sheriff's department that we could go to with this?"

Cameron shook his head. "No. It all starts and ends with Sheriff Odette."

"He has to report to someone, though," said Jasmin.

"Well, there is the county judge two towns over. He's the only person the sheriff ultimately answered to, but he's out of town until mid-next week."

"Of course he is," said Jasmin. "Welcome to Smallville, USA."

"Well, we can't wait that long," said Torie. "Who knows what could happen to Emily during that time."

"Agreed," said Jasmin. "What are our next steps?"

Torie arched an eyebrow. "So much for staying on the sidelines with this one, huh?"

"There's something crooked here," replied Jasmin. "And you know how I feel about that."

"Cameron, where is the jail they would be keeping Emily at? I think we need to pay her a visit. There's more to her than meets the eye, and I think it's time we find out just what she knows."

"Well, there's only one cell in town. It's built onto the back of Trevor Pine's auto body shop."

Torie could hardly contain her laughter.

"Wait a second. Trevor is the town mechanic, postmaster general, and jailer? What more can happen in this town?"

"Girl, hush," said Jasmin, "you know better than to put things like that out there. Let's go see Emily, and while we're there we can check on the car too. Something tells me we might be needing to get out of this town faster than expected."

Chapter Eleven

They found Trevor working in the garage. The large space was immaculate, with an array of specialty tools arranged along one entire wall of the shop. The other wall was covered with metallic rolling carts with red drawers. A roll-up steel door allowed cars of all shape and size to be driven into the space and parked on a lift above a generous opening with a ladder leading down into the pit for easy access to the undercarriage of the autos.

They found Trevor standing along the tool wall, clipboard in hand, comparing what he was seeing on his wall with what was marked on the board. He turned as he heard their approach.

"Well, hello, ladies. If you're here about your car, I haven't received the parts yet, but I did confirm that they will be here earlier than I expected. So, you know what that means?" He offered a big smile. "It means you'll be out of here much sooner than you expected."

"Well, that's excellent news," said Jasmin. Her tone was

a little more chipper than Torie was expecting, especially given what they had just learned.

"Thank you so much, Trevor," Torie added. "But that's really not what we are here about."

Trevor put down his clipboard and wiped his hands on a towel that hung on a rack below the tools before making his way over to the two women.

"Oh yeah? What can I do for you?"

"Well," started Jasmin, "It's come to our attention that you wear yet another cap in this town?"

He looked at them, confusion creeping across his face before it brightened.

"Oh, you mean the jail thing? Yeah, that isn't my thing. I just lease the space to Sheriff Odette."

"So, you're not the jailer?" asked Jasmin.

"Well, not exactly. Certainly not officially. But someone has to keep an eye on anyone who gets thrown in. I get a small stipend to keep an eye on the prisoners, bring them food, make sure everything is okay with them until they get released. And honestly, it doesn't happen that often. Usually it's just Marvin, the town drunk, who gets tossed in every now and then to sleep one off."

"But if it's just you, who keeps an eye on them at night?" Torie asked.

"I still pop down. My apartment is just above the jail space on the back of the shop here." He jabbed his thumb over his shoulder.

"Of course you do. So much for that idea," said Jasmin, under her breath.

"What was that?" Trevor asked.

"Oh, she didn't say anything," said Torie, shooting a side eye to her friend. "So we heard that you have a...visitor in the jail now."

"Oh, you mean Emily? Yes, she's in there. Gotta say, I was surprised at that. Wasn't expecting her to turn out to be a murderer," Trevor said, shaking his head.

"Alleged murderer," said Jasmin. "Why are certain people in this town so quick to jump to conclusions?"

"Well, if you ask me, and you did, it's because of the whole occult thing she's into. You can't practice black magic and not be willing to kill," he replied matter-of-factly.

"Well, to be fair, we were in her store, and I didn't see anything that looked like black magic," said Jasmin.

"Not that we know what black magic looks like," Torie interjected. "But it seemed like everything she was doing was all natural—crystals, candles, healing potions. Not that we believe in it of course."

"Well, you tell that to Miss Krissy. See if she agrees at just how helpful Emily's potions are," Trevor replied.

"Krissy? Are you talking about the lady who owns the organic pet shop?" Torie asked.

"Yes, that's her. She doesn't like to talk about it, but you know she was married once. Happily. She owned a large farm just outside of town that she and her husband were planning to turn into a shelter for abused animals.

"Well, turns out, her husband ended up leaving her and took everything. He hooked up with this crooked lady lawyer from Beaumont, and they were able to get everything from Krissy in the divorce, and then they sold the land so they could leave high and mighty. Now, Krissy has had to start over again, and is trying to save up enough money to buy back the land that she already owned. It's a crying shame," he said, shaking his head.

Jasmin frowned. "But what does that have to do with Emily?"

"The lawyer who stole Krissy's husband used a love

potion she got from Emily on him. That's how she was able to get her hooks into him," Trevor said, his eyes widening.

Jasmin clucked her tongue. "Or maybe, he wasn't too invested in the marriage to begin with. Love is one of the most powerful forces in creation; a simple potion can't sap it. Or so I've heard."

Trevor cocked his head to one side. "You're a funny pair, you know that?"

Torie just smiled, not quite sure what he meant by funny.

"In any event, I was wondering if it would be possible for us to talk to Emily," she said.

"Sure you can," he replied happily. "As long as you get the sheriff's permission first. Then I'll be happy to let you see her."

Yeah, cos something tells me the sheriff is going to let us talk to the one person who could probably put him out of a job...or worse, thought Torie.

"Oh, I wasn't sure what the process was. I mean, we just wanted to drop in to speak to her quickly. She was so nice to us, we just wanted to see if she needed anything," Torie said. "It would only take a minute."

Trevor twisted his mouth in thought, and she could almost hear the back-and-forth internal dialogue he was having.

"Look, y'all seem like good people, but I can't do that. The sheriff would have my head if I broke protocol. But I'm sure if you talk to him first, he would be more than happy to let you see her for a minute."

Torie debated telling him she wasn't sure how well that would work, as her mind began chewing through ideas on what to do next. Of course, having a partner in crime had made her next move considerably easier.

"So this is very fascinating," said Jasmin out of the blue. "You're able to work on all engine types from here? How did you learn how to use all these tools?" She waved her hand at the wall and casually walked over to them.

Before Trevor could answer, her left leg shot out in front of her in a jerky movement and at the same time she grabbed her back.

"Aw, oh no, my back. I think I slipped on something on the floor!" she said, grimacing in pain.

Immediately, Trevor rushed to her side, rushing to place an arm around her for support.

"Oh, no. Are you okay, Jasmin? What can I do?"

Jasmin made a show of grabbing at her back, her face tightening with pain.

"I just have a bad back that I have to be careful with. It goes out on me from time to time."

"I am so sorry. What can I do?"

"I...I just need to lay flat on a firm, but not too hard surface for a few minutes. Let the spasm die down. Do you have a bench or hard couch...?"

"Yes, sure. Let me help you to my office; there's a couch in there that should be just what you need."

"Thank you. I can't thank you enough. I'm being such a pain I know." She shot a look at Torie over her shoulder.

"I'll run out front and see how fast I can get a ride for us, maybe find an ice pack for your back. I'll be right back!" she said, rushing from the garage.

"Hey, I have ice—" started Trevor. He was stopped by Jasmin's sudden spasm.

"Oh, let her go. She doesn't handle crisis situations very well. I'll be okay in just a few, if you can just help me lie down for a minute before it completely locks up."

Trevor carefully lifted her arm and put it around his

neck as he led her out of the garage space and towards a door that led to his office. As they entered, Jasmin chanced a glance behind her where she could see Torie doubling back around and heading for the makeshift jail station Trevor had pointed out.

Torie found the brick and wood, two-story addition that jutted off the back of Trevor's auto shop. She could tell it had been an older structure that was modified to suit his current needs, as the lower level had only one locked door as an entry point, with no windows along the back side.

Stairs led to the upper level, which looked more like an apartment, with nice windows and flower boxes adorning the backside.

She made her way to the door, giving the handle a turn, even though she knew it would not be open. There was no time for subtlety, so she forced her magic into the lock, popping it open.

Inside, she was greeted by a small outer room with a desk and spindly wooden chair. Behind that, there was a doorway leading into a darker space, with only the faintest glow of light showing through.

"Emily," she said in a forceful whisper, "are you in here?"

"I'm back here!" came a call from the other side of the opening.

Torie followed her voice until she came to a single room with iron bars where there should have been a door. Inside the cell, on a tiny cot secured to the wall, sat Emily. She was so small that her feet didn't touch the floor and instead were swinging to and fro like a child on a playground swing.

"Emily are you alright?" asked Torie, rushing to the bars.

"I'm fine...how did you get back here? Did you find the drive I left?"

"Yes, we found it, but I don't have a lot of time. Are you in danger? Does the sheriff know what you found?"

"He has an idea, yes. I don't know how he found out. I don't think I'm in danger. At least not that I know of."

"How did you get those records?" Torie asked.

"The drive was sent to me by someone anonymously. I don't know who it was or why they sent it to me."

Torie looked at the locking mechanism on the cell door. It didn't look like it would put up too much of a fight. Emily glanced up, sensing something was amiss.

"No, don't," she said.

"Don't what?" said Torie.

"Don't do whatever it is you're about to do. Which I'm guessing is probably the same thing you did to get in here."

Torie narrowed her eyes as she regarded the woman.

"Emily, how did you know to put up that cloaking spell inside your store?"

"I didn't," came the answer. "The stone I used was one that was resonated at a protection frequency. When I placed it, all I would do was focus my will on hoping it would keep everything in my shop safe. I don't know how to cast actual spells. Unlike you, I presume."

Torie glanced around, aware that Jasmin's ruse could end at any moment and Trevor could come storming in. She was torn on how to answer the query. Sure, there were normal humans in Singing Falls who knew what she was capable of, but they were part of the community; affiliated with the supernatural aspect of the town in some way.

But this wasn't Singing Falls, and she didn't know Emily. Even though something in the back of her mind told her she could trust this woman; even with a pending murder charge hanging over her head.

"And your presumption would be correct. I can get you out of here."

Again, Emily shook her head. "That would only cement my guilt in Odette's mind. If you want to help me, find out who emailed that flash drive to me and find Samantha's real killer."

"Emily, what does the sheriff have on you? He wouldn't make an arrest like this without something."

Emily took a deep breath and exhaled slowly.

"He said that Samantha looked like she had been poisoned. At least that's what the coroner said. And at the scene they found a couple of medicine jars from my shop, putting me in the area."

"Were you there?"

She nodded. "I was. But only to collect some of the rarer herbs that grow wild there. I use them in the candles I make and some of my healing potions. But I didn't kill anyone. I didn't even see or hear anything. But he's saying that Samantha's bloodwork will probably come back matching the samples of my herbs in the jars they found. I told him that wasn't possible, but he seemed to think other-wise. At the very least, he said he's got me on trespassing and can hold me for forty-eight hours on that. That's plenty of time for him to get the coroners statement and lab work certified."

"I smell a set-up," Torie said.

"And just what makes you think that? And how did you get in here?"

Torie turned to see Sheriff Odette standing in the space behind her. His arms were folded across his massive chest, and he leveled Torie with a look that she could only describe as dark and stormy.

Chapter Twelve

Torie cursed herself for not having erected a ward behind her to alert her to any intrusion. Her mind raced, thinking of over a dozen spells she could cast that would have handled the situation. She pushed those away, opting for another route.

"Oh, hello, Sheriff," she said, forcing a quick smile. "We were just checking on our car with Trevor when Jasmin hurt her back. Trevor was just helping her out, and I decided to come by and see how Emily was doing. The door was open, and I didn't think anything about just coming on in."

"The door was unlocked?" he said, and a frown darkened his features even more. "I'll have to have a talk with Trevor about that."

Darn, thought Torie, realizing too late that she had probably just put the mechanic's job in jeopardy. Or at least one of his jobs.

"But you're not allowed in here without my permission or an escort; and also, what's this talk about a set-up?"

Torie mulled the answers she could give over in her head and decided to tackle the situation head on.

"Sheriff, has this woman had access to her lawyer yet?"

"Not just yet…I'm still processing her."

"Well, that's fine, but I understand you've also been questioning her without her lawyer being present. You know that's considered a denial of due process and rights."

She saw the big sheriff's jaw tighten and could practically hear his teeth grinding. She had no idea if what she was saying was true, but she seemed to remember a lot of this from watching the nearly endless episodes of *Law and Order*.

"I was just offering Emily the use of my personal lawyer. He practices in New York, but I was just saying that I am sure he could provide a very good referral for West Virginia, and she should really take him up on it because without a lawyer, you are setting yourself up for all kinds of problems. Right, Emily?"

Emily bobbed her head up and down spiritedly.

"Well, that's all fine and good," he replied, relaxing his stance just a little. "But the fact is, we booked her on trespassing and are looking at a possible connection between her and the victim. Which I am not allowed to go into, as you can imagine. We are holding her for forty-eight hours, and then she will be free to contact her lawyer."

Torie knew not to press her luck. She had probably already gotten poor Trevor fired, and she had a feeling her presence here had not endeared her and Jasmin to the sheriff either.

"Well, I'm sorry for butting in. I certainly wouldn't want to interfere in an investigation in any way. I should probably be getting back to my friend; see how she's doing."

"Yes. Why don't you do that," said Sheriff Odette. "I'll

have a quick word with Ms. Belmont." He stepped forward, extending an arm to usher Torie out of the room.

"Thank you, Sheriff," she said before turning to Emily one last time. "I'll reach out to my lawyer and have a name for you in a couple of days when they can see you, okay?"

She watched as Emily slowly nodded, and then, acting on impulse, she shot a thought at the woman.

"Don't worry. Jasmin and I are going to look into this. We're going to get you out of here. Nod if you understand."

A hopeful look crossed Emily's face, but she nodded once, and Torie turned to leave the enclosed space.

Hurrying out of the building, Torie made her way back into the garage, and found Jasmin lying on the small couch in Trevor's office while he raced back and forth, worriedly, in front of her.

"Are you sure there isn't more I can do for you, ma'am? We do have a really good doctor in town. Let me give her a call, she'll come right over," Trevor was saying.

"What, you mean you're not the town physician as well?" Torie said as she approached.

It was an attempt to make Trevor laugh, but it didn't work. She felt bad about tricking him, and she felt even worse that he was about to catch the wrath of Sheriff Odette for something he had no part in.

"Jasmin, are you feeling well enough to get going? I called for a rideshare and it's a way off, but you know how it always helps loosen your back up to walk some. We really shouldn't take up any more of Trevor's time."

That last sentence was a little more pointed, and Jasmin nodded, slowly sitting up off the couch, careful not to grimace too much.

"You know, you're right. A good walk will probably do me a world of good. I feel like such a goof lying here like this, when this man probably has so much work to get caught up on."

Trevor frowned, stretching out a hand to help her up.

"Ma'am, are you sure? You are in so much pain."

"Story of my life," Jasmin said with a smile. "But really, like I said, I just needed a quick minute to take the pressure off my lower back. I'll be fine. Happened to me before and I'm sure it will happen again."

She hooked her arm through Torie's, and together they headed for the door.

"What happened?" she asked in a whisper, leaning in so that only Torie could hear her.

"Sheriff Odette is here! We need to go. Now. I'll fill you in on the rest once we are away."

Jasmin arched her eyebrows and made it a point to pick up her shuffling pace, leaving a confused Trevor to stand there scratching his head.

"I'll call you as soon as I start the repairs," he called after them.

"No problem, take your time," said Torie, waving one hand goodbye over her head.

Once they were away from the garage, and out of Trevor's line of sight, they hurried along, heading for Main Street.

"Did the Sheriff see you?" asked Jasmin.

"Oh yeah. And I may have gotten Trevor in a bit of trouble with him, but at least I got to see Emily."

"And?"

"Well, she's not a witch after all," Torie said.

"What? Of course she isn't. I could have told you that if you had asked."

"But I was able to confirm there is more to her than she

presents. She is definitely psychically attuned. Maybe a low-level telepath…or an empath, maybe."

"Did she tell you why she was the suspect in a murder investigation?"

Torie quickly repeated the conversation she had with Emily as they made their way to Cameron's coffee shop.

"If we figure out who sent her the flash drive, then we are one step closer to finding out who may have killed Samantha," Torie said.

"Torie, we need to be careful here. These aren't super-naturals we are dealing with. We can't just cast a revelation spell or bend them to our will." Jasmin paused, looking at her friend. "Or maybe we could. I mean, messing around with a human mind is tricky, but it can be done. If we cast the right spell, we could solve this by lunch. We could just use a little Jedi mind whammy."

Torie thought about it but shook her head. Something about that just didn't feel right.

"No. Self-defense is one thing; but I don't want to start down a path of manipulating minds to get what we want."

Jasmin smiled, placing her arm around her friend.

"You're growing, my little Padawan learner."

"I…have no idea what that is," Torie said.

Jasmin stopped mid-stride, looking at Torie like she had two heads.

"What? Do I have something in my teeth?" Torie asked.

"You seriously don't know what a Padawan is? What did you think I was referencing when I said Jedi mind whammy?"

"Honestly, I thought it was just some kind of hex magic I wasn't familiar with."

Jasmin shook her head sadly. "Someone has seriously failed your education. But don't worry; we are going to correct that as soon as we get back. There's a *Star Wars* marathon night in your future."

Torie wasn't exactly sure what she meant by it but had to admit it sounded more appealing than a naked weekend with Elric.

They stood outside the coffee shop, looking through the window at the small line that had formed inside.

"Should we get another coffee? Cameron might be able to tell us some more about the goings on with the Perry family. Maybe point us in the right direction as to who could have sent that information to Emily," said Jasmin.

"I don't know. I mean, we already got Trevor in trouble. I don't want to drag anyone else into this. Besides, why ask him when we can just go back to The Sweetbriar and go right to the all-knowing source?"

Jasmin looked at Torie in confusion, before understanding spread across her face.

"Kitty, the tell-all maid."

Torie nodded with a smile. "Something tells me we won't need a mind whammy to get information out of that one."

They arrived back at The Sweetbriar to find a very somber atmosphere. Granted, there had been a murder committed on the grounds, but the air seemed heavier than when they left. Kitty was in the large kitchen, as usual, slowly going through the motions of unpacking boxes of groceries and placing them in the cabinets.

"Kitty, what's going on?" asked Torie.

The woman looked up, her eyes tearful.

"The Henrys. They said they are going to sell The

Sweetbriar to the Perrys. They don't have the money to fight off the lawsuits they are being threatened with."

Torie exhaled sharply, placing a hand on Kitty's shoulder and squeezing gently.

"I just don't know what we are going to do," said Kitty. "This inn supports a lot of people. Now, we are all looking at losing our jobs. I guess this is just the world we are moving to. Those that have, will take; those that need, will suffer."

Torie felt a flood of resolve move through her. There was a sense of finality in Kitty's tone that Torie refused to accept. She wasn't sure how, but every instinct she had told her that the issues here were intertwined.

If she could solve one, the other would follow.

Chapter Thirteen

Jasmin pulled out a chair at the large, eat-in table that was used as a prep station in the kitchen, and beckoned for Kitty to take a seat. The poor woman was clearly distraught; her hands trembled as she raised them to her face.

Torie hurried to the self-serve station, pouring a cup of tea and placing it in front of Kitty.

"I am so sorry this is happening," said Torie. "I can only imagine what you must be feeling."

"It…it's not just me. I'm worried about what this will do for the town. This is a large piece of leverage they will acquire; the rest of the business owners will see this, and they'll fold. It's the beginning of the end."

"Well, not yet it isn't," said Jasmin. "The deal isn't done yet, so that means there is still hope."

Torie pulled out a chair and sat across from the two women. Her hand was warm and comforting as she wrapped it around Kitty's.

"Kitty, we don't think Emily was the one responsible for Samantha Perry's death. And I think if we can find the real killer, it may help change the outcome of what is happening here."

The maid sniffed, looking at the two of them with pleading eyes.

"How will that stop anything?" she implored.

Torie took a deep breath. "Well, it could change the narrative and the playing field if...and I hesitate to say this...someone closer to Samantha was the one who killed her."

Kitty's eyes widened. "You don't think one of her own family did this, do you?"

"I think that anyone who would do something like this had something to gain. What did Emily have to gain?"

"I heard the sheriff talking to the Henrys after he made the arrest. He said they have physical evidence that puts her at the crime scene, and they had other evidence that connected her to it as well.

"The Henrys said that while it was a tragedy, that would mean the Perrys don't really have a lawsuit. But Sheriff Odette said that it still happened on their property and that the Perrys are saying it happened as a result of negligence on the part of the Henrys. They shouldn't let the guests wander around the springs like they do without someone watching over them. It's like having a public swimming pool and no lifeguard on duty, or something like that."

Torie frowned, casting a glance in Jasmin's direction. She could tell her friend was thinking the same thing. It sounded like the sheriff was supplying a narrative that helped push the Perrys' agenda. The question was why?

"Kitty, do you know of any connection the sheriff might have to the Perrys?" said Jasmin.

Kitty thought for a moment, sipping her tea. "No, not that I know of."

"How long has he been the sheriff here?" asked Torie.

"Oh, Ben grew up here from what I've heard. He's a fixture of this town. He may be a little rough around the edges, but he's a good man."

"Does he have any relatives in the area?" asked Jasmin.

"Just an aunt who raised him. But she passed away a few years back. Such a shame. She was a beautiful woman; she was killed in a hit and run over on Lawyers Road." She clucked her tongue, shaking her head slowly with the memory.

"What about any other connections the Perrys may have with the townsfolk? I take it they aren't very well liked."

"Oh, they are pretty much hated, as you can imagine. If you're looking for motive, then you'd have a list that included half the town. But maybe start with that guy who works at the coffee shop."

A jolt passed through both Torie and Jasmin, their backs going ramrod straight at her words.

"You mean Cameron?" asked Jasmin. "Why would he be involved?"

"Well, for starters, the Perrys purchased the supply company that supplies his coffee. They have tripled the prices and delivery fees trying to force him to sell his shop. From what I hear, he's close to having his house foreclosed on, and the strain has driven him and his husband to near divorce. He was here just before the two of you showed up, and I heard him arguing with Samantha about how unfair it was what they were doing." She lowered her voice and leaned in closer to the women. "I heard him say he wasn't going to feel bad when she got what she had coming to her."

No one said anything as Torie and Jasmin stared at one another.

"I guess the Perrys really want to develop downtown," Torie said, trying not to think too deeply about what Kitty had just told them.

"What about the Perrys themselves?" asked Jasmin. "You mentioned before that they are not a tight-knit family. Do you know why?"

"No one specific thing. But I do know the brother and his wife are constantly having these little...moments. She's always crying, and he's always snapping at her for some reason. And it got worse after Samantha's death."

"Anything else come to mind?" said Torie. "This has all been very helpful."

Kitty shook her head. "Um, you know, I hope you don't think I'm just spreading idle gossip. I wouldn't want to get in any trouble with the Henrys."

Torie clapped the back of Kitty's hand. "Not at all. And this all stays between us."

Kitty offered an understanding smile. "Thank you. I appreciate that. Now, if you'll excuse me, I need to finish putting all these away, and then I'm going to take some tea up to Mrs. Henry. She's taking all of this pretty hard."

She pushed her chair back and headed back to her work, leaving Torie and Jasmin to stew on all that she had said.

Together, they headed up the stairs to Torie's room. Jasmin shut the door behind her and slumped against it.

"You don't think Cameron had anything to do with this, do you?" she asked.

Torie shrugged her shoulders. "I can't imagine he would, right? I mean, he has such a nice smile."

"So did Ted Bundy," Jasmin groaned.

"Well, I think if we show up at that coffee shop again, great smile or no, we will have worn out our stay, and I'm sure he's going to get suspicious."

"Well, then why don't we invite him here?" suggested Jasmin. "We can treat him to a fancy dinner here at the inn as a way of saying thank you for all the free drinks and for his help with the…flash drive." The last part she only mouthed.

"That's actually a good idea. He will be a little more off guard if he's not on his own home turf. We might be able to get some more out of him. In the meantime, I think it's time to start spending a little more time with the grieving family."

"Well, it's only proper that we express our condolences."

"Should we divide and conquer?" Torie asked. "It might seem less like an inquisition if we don't double team them."

"Maybe. But at the same time, it might seem more natural if we just bumped into them since we are usually seen together anyway."

The sound of a door slamming, followed by extremely loud voices filtered through the wall, drawing their attention. Torie opened the door, and they stuck their heads out, just in time to see Millie Perry storming down the hall from the opposite wing, closely pursued by her husband, Jacob. He was trying to grab her by the arm to stop her, but she wasn't having it, shaking off his attempts.

"Millie, enough of this. We need to have each other's backs right now!" he said harshly.

"Oh, is that what you were having with Samantha? Her back?" his wife replied angrily.

Jacob's face turned a deep crimson as he grabbed his wife, spinning her to face him.

Just then, Torie and Jasmin stepped into the hallway, making their presence known.

"Everything okay here?" asked Jasmin, giving Jacob a look that dared him to continue acting the way he was.

"Just a...family matter," Jacob said. He coughed to clear his throat and eased his grip on Millie, finally releasing the woman and stepping back. "Millie, I'll see you back in our room." He took a step back before shuffling towards his room.

Millie remained standing, her back stiff until she heard the door to their suite close. Her shoulders slumped and she dropped her face to her hands.

Jasmin rushed forward, putting her arm around the shoulders of the shorter woman and gently leading her into Torie's room. They sat her on the small sofa in the sitting area and handed her some tissues.

They let her cry it out, providing silent support until she was ready to speak. Sometimes, family can hurt one another far more than any stranger, and the only salve for a wound that deep was a good, ugly cry.

Torie took the tissues from her and discarded them.

"Can we get you anything?" she asked.

Millie huffed before looking up with red, puffy eyes. "I don't suppose you have a bottle of bourbon in here anywhere, do you?"

The witches laughed, and Torie briefly wondered if she could indeed conjure a bottle out of thin air, but then thought better of the urge to try it.

"No bourbon, but I can certainly call for a bottle of wine to be sent up," said Jasmin.

Millie shook her head. Her close-cropped curls were firmly set in place and refused to move.

"No, please. I was only kidding. Well, half kidding. But thank you for the offer."

Torie gave her a moment and then spoke up.

"I'm sure, whatever that was, it wasn't something you want to talk about, but if you feel the need to, we are a judgement-free zone."

Millie nodded and looked at the women. Her exhalation was as weak as the smile she managed.

"Men. I don't understand them," she said. "I mean, I'm no beauty, but…we made promises to one another so many years ago. And now look…"

Torie and Jasmin exchanged hard looks.

"I don't know what happened, though I can guess from what little we heard," said Torie. "If it helps, I've been where you are right now."

Millie's head snapped up; her mouth slightly agape. She looked like she was about to say something, but then swallowed her words, her eyes falling to her feet.

"I feel so ashamed. I don't know what I did to deserve this," she said.

Torie felt anger cause her face to flush. Not anger at the woman; but the person or persons that had shaped her to feel responsible for the bad decisions that crappy people made. Personally, she was all too familiar with what Millie was going through. How many times had she lain awake at night with those pesky questions that started with 'W' keeping her awake?

Why had she not done something sooner to make him happy?

What did she have that Torie didn't?

What could she have done better?

Why wasn't she good enough?

It almost ate her alive. And it took time for her to really accept that her ex-husband's shortfalls had nothing to do with her. Sure, things hadn't always been perfect between them, but she hadn't been the one to throw everything away. It wasn't until she let go of all the 'W' questions that she was able to find peace.

"Don't say that," Torie said. "You can only take responsibility for you; it's up to him to do the same."

"I just...I mean, why her, of all people? She's awful." Millie stopped short, her eyes welling up. "Was. She *was* awful." The tears started again, and she reached for another tissue from the box. "Honestly, I don't know if I'm crying for me or for her. We were friends. Not just in-laws. And she goes and does this."

Jasmin placed a hand on Millie's shoulder and began to rub her back in support.

"Can I ask," said Torie, "when did you find out?"

Millie took a deep breath before looking up at her. "I had my suspicions for a while that it was...someone. Someone else. But then, just yesterday, he told me. At the same time, she told Walter; her husband and Jacob's brother. They had it planned. Turns out that was the real reason we came here." She chuckled, shaking her head. "I wondered why she was so intent on coming here to have this business meeting." She placed air-quotes around the word meeting as it was spat from her mouth. "I mean, we've been discussing this buy and ways to squeeze the locals into signing off on this for months now. I knew she had her agenda, but I didn't think it included stealing my husband as well."

Torie straightened, latching onto her words.

"What do you mean by agenda?" she asked.

"Samantha was using her majority share to call off the deal. Something had changed her mind about developing in this town. She and Jacob were cashing out and leaving the family business. They were starting over together, away from all of this—and us."

Jasmin's eyes were wide as she regarded her friend.

"And she told this to her husband yesterday?" she enquired.

Millie nodded. "At the same time Jacob told me. Yesterday morning."

"So as far as the company goes, she was calling the shots?" asked Torie.

"Yes. The seed money to start the development business came from her father. Of course, Walter and Jacob grew the business into what it is now, but the start-up money was hers. That was why her father made sure that she always had a majority vote."

"So, if she had indeed followed through on what she intended, how would it have hurt the family business?" asked Torie.

Millie pursed her lips. "Honestly, it would have nearly bankrupted the company. Walter had sunk so much into this particular deal that it would have been hard to recover. He was banking on a massive payout when the developers bought in."

Torie looked at Jasmin and could tell her friend was thinking the exact same thoughts as her. For the super wealthy, there was nothing scarier than losing it all.

Money could make people do all kinds of things outside their normal boundaries.

Even kill.

Chapter Fourteen

Once Millie had put her emotions back into her carefully crafted bottle, she had excused herself and left the two witches alone.

"Wow," said Jasmin. "That was some serious family drama."

"No kidding. I feel bad for Millie, but I think she just gave us another suspect. If Walter knew what his wife was planning before she was murdered…"

"Actually, she gave us two suspects," said Jasmin.

"What? You think Jacob could have killed her? He was ready to leave his marriage for her."

"Probably not him, but I'm thinking of Millie. She said they were more than just in-laws, they were friends. The hurt she must have felt was twofold. So, I say we consider her and Walter."

"He had motive and certainly opportunity. I mean, for all we know, he could have been with Samantha at the mineral pond and that's where she told him what was going on."

"So now we add them to the mix with the sheriff. This is getting deep. But there is still one more piece we need to look at."

"What's that?" asked Torie.

"We need to find out what Samantha's agenda was that Millie mentioned. What could have made her abandon the plans for developing this town? I'm thinking it wasn't just love. No, something else must have happened, and we need to find out what it was."

"Well, the only person who knows that is Samantha. Should we try calling on her spirit and compelling it to speak with us?" suggested Torie.

"What? No, girl. We don't have the time to properly secure the inn for raising spirits. But she wasn't the only one who knew; whatever they were planning, Jacob was in on it as well."

"Okay, but is it okay if we go a little rough on him? He really has it coming."

Jasmin smiled. "I like the way you think. But first things first. We need to speak with Cameron and find out where he was during all of this."

Torie had her phone out and her fingers were deftly fluttering over the surface of it.

"I left a message on his work line with my number, telling him yo meet us at seven. No excuses," she said. No sooner had the words left her mouth than there was a ding. "He's in." She slipped the phone back into her bag and turned to face Jasmin.

"I have to say, this is turning out to be a really fun vacation. You were right, we needed to get involved," said Jasmin.

"Jasmin. Someone is dead. This isn't fun."

"Oh, you're right. Of course not. But, if you think

about it, if we weren't here, she would still be dead. And a potentially innocent woman would be taking the fall for it."

Torie wrinkled her brow. "True. But we still shouldn't be relishing the situation."

Jasmin looked at her, her features growing heavy.

"What is it?" asked Torie. "I didn't mean to hurt your feelings."

"Ha. No, you didn't. I was just thinking about how awful this will end up being if Cameron were the killer. I mean, he's so beautiful. And I was already thinking about when we come back to visit—"

"Oh, so now we're coming back at some point?" said Torie.

Jasmin lifted her shoulders, leaning her head to one side.

"I mean...as long as it doesn't become one big strip mall, I think I could handle coming back here again. But we have to bring Fionna. Can you imagine how much she would fall in love with this place?"

The mention of their friend caused images of Leo to flash into Torie's mind. She wondered what the little dragon was up to. Was he eating? Did he miss her? Were dragons capable of missing their humans? For that matter, was she his human or just someone who fed and sheltered him until he was big enough to go off on his own, looking for lands to pillage?

And thinking about Leo inevitably led her to think about Elric. She missed the wolf so much, she ached thinking about him. Hearing Millie lament about what she was going through had opened old wounds Torie had thought were long scabbed over.

Her ex-husband had used her and cast her aside much the same way as Millie's. Torie could only hope that Millie would come out of this stronger for it. That she too would find her tribe.

Of course, the difference was that when Millie found her tribe, Torie doubted it would be a supernatural community that helped her usher in magical powers the likes of which she could never imagine.

"...Hello," Jasmin was snapping her fingers in front of Torie's face to bring her back to reality. "Torie, stop! Wake up!"

"What? Oh, I'm sorry, Jasmin. My mind was wandering."

Jasmin grasped Torie's hand and held it up.

"I'd say you were wandering all right."

Torie looked at her hand and gasped. It was sparkling as the magic that flowed within her moved up and down her limbs, making her almost translucent. She shook her head, calling to her magic, drawing it back inside and calming the flow.

"What was that?" she asked, shocked.

"You were about to drift," said Jasmin. "I've read about it, but never actually seen it. It's when witches can move from one point in space to another, without creating a teleportation spell. Their mind drifts to a place and their body follows. It's very dangerous. Where were you going?"

"I...I don't know. I wasn't going anywhere; I mean, I was thinking about Leo and Elric and how much I missed them. Why is it so dangerous?"

Jasmin sat back, studying her friend.

"It is dangerous because you have no anchor. Your mind wanders, and the body follows. But sometimes, the body doesn't end up where the mind is; you can lose your footing, so to speak, and rematerialize anywhere. You could appear on a crowded freeway in oncoming traffic, or inside a wall. I once read about a witch who drifted next to a river and her mind flowed with the current until she appeared at the bottom of an inlet. Or…"

"Or what?" Torie demanded when Jasmin didn't continue.

"Or you could be one of those drifters who specialize in bilocation. Meaning your body can appear in two places at once, but your mind only stays with one. And if that one gets lost, then the remaining you is simply a comatose vessel; forever."

Torie shuddered. "How do you control it? What exactly is an anchor?"

"When we cast a teleportation spell, like we did once before, your anchor is the point from which you vanish. That is where you drop anchor, so to speak. If something happens and you get lost, you would be snapped back to that point in space.

"As for how you control it…you control your mind. Don't let it slip away; especially not with the kind of power you possess."

"I'm sorry. I guess I still have a lot to learn."

Jasmin softened. "Don't apologize. You can't help something that you didn't know about. I personally have never possessed the ability to drift; so, it never occurred to me to warn you about it. Live and learn."

"Does an anchor have to be a place?" Torie asked.

Jasmin mulled the question over before giving her a confused look. "I'm not sure. I suppose it could be an object."

"Or a person?" asked Torie, giving her a conspiratorial look.

"We will talk about that once we are back in Singing

Falls. But for now, keep your mind here and present. Got it?"

Torie nodded.

"So back to the game plan with Cameron. Why don't we ask Kitty to arrange a nice dinner on the upper Terrace? It's quieter there, and I don't want him running into any of the Perrys if we can avoid it," she said.

"Sounds like a good plan. In the meantime, why don't we have a chat with Jacob? See if he knows anything."

"And maybe let him know that it's not nice to put your hands on a woman..." added Torie.

———

The younger of the Perry brothers wasn't hard to find. He was sitting at a table on the lower terrace, overlooking the grounds, swirling a glass of dark liquor in a way that caused the ice cubes to clink rhythmically.

He saw Torie and Jasmin approaching and looked about nervously before locking eyes with the two witches.

"Look, I don't know what you thought you saw up there, but it wasn't—"

Torie held up a hand, cutting the man off.

"First, let me start by saying I am sorry for your loss," she said.

Her words startled Jacob slightly, throwing him off balance.

"Thank you," he said, warily. "I...wasn't expecting that."

"Now having said that, you do know that your wife was entitled to her own reaction in the wake of the news you dropped on her, right? What wasn't appropriate was your reaction to her feelings," said Jasmin.

Jacob bristled, clearing his throat as he attempted to stand up.

"Uh-uh," said Jasmin. Her eyes flashed for a brief second, and Jacob found himself roughly pushed back into his chair by something he couldn't see. "We aren't easily intimidated. I suggest you remain seated while we talk."

The look of shock in his eyes turned to fear as the women stepped closer, standing over the man. He attempted to struggle against the invisible bonds that held him, but then stopped when Jasmin held up a finger and wiggled it from side to side.

"I was wrong to grab her like that," he said hastily. "You gotta believe me when I say I've never put my hands on her before, and I regret having done it today. And even though I'm pretty sure our marriage is over, it will never happen again."

Torie cocked her head to one side, letting her magic caress the words that came from his mouth.

"I believe you," she said. "But if it's all the same to you, we'd like to ask you a couple of questions."

Jacob tensed and started to sit forward, feeling the bonds that held him soften and dissipate. He looked down at his arms, which he was now able to lift and then up at the two women.

"What…how did you do that?" he asked.

"Hypnotic suggestion," Jasmin said, smiling and then laughing at the puzzled look on the man's face. "Don't worry about it; just be thankful that we didn't teach Millie how it works."

Torie's smile mirrored Jasmin's as she saw him shiver inwardly. "Jacob, there is no easy way to ask this, but how long have you been having an affair with your sister-in-law?"

Again, the man flinched, his jaw setting. "What business is that of yours? What, are you attorneys? Looking to latch onto my wife for a settlement? She will be just fine, I assure you."

"Let's just say that our concerns lie with making sure Emily Belmont doesn't take the fall for something she didn't do," said Jasmin.

Jacob's face wrinkled then hardened. "Belmont? The woman who killed Samantha? She'll get what she has coming to her I hope. And after all I did for her."

That last remark didn't escape Torie. "What did you do for her? And if she is the one who killed Samantha, then yes, justice needs to be done. But if she didn't do it…and I don't think she did, we need to make sure she isn't found guilty."

"And just as importantly, we need to make sure the real killer is found," added Jasmin.

Torie took in the man sitting before them. She could see from the way he regarded them and the set of his jaw, that he wasn't really buying what they were saying.

"Or we could not get involved at all," she said, "just leave this to play out naturally. Whoever was bold enough to kill her and get away with it might not stop at one Perry. Especially if word gets out that her secret lover might know something about what caused her to be a target in the first place."

Jasmin nodded slowly, pointing her finger at Torie. "You're right. Maybe we should wait this out; see what happens. I mean, we are uniquely qualified to deal with things like this, but hey…I'm sure the local sheriff will provide plenty of protection for the rest of the Perrys."

At the mention of the sheriff, Jacob stiffened considerably, even as the two women turned to walk away.

"No wait!" he said. "You think...I might be in danger?"

Torie shrugged. "No way of knowing. If you're one hundred percent certain that Emily killed your lover, then you're fine. If not..." She let her words trail off menacingly.

"Okay, look, I'll tell you what I can, but you have to keep my name out of any blowback. Agreed?"

"Agreed," said Torie, hurrying to sit opposite the man before he changed his mind. "Let's start with the sheriff. Why does he make you so jumpy? What does he do for your family? We know he's on the family payroll."

Jacob looked genuinely confused. "What are you talking about? Ben Odette isn't on any payroll."

"We saw proof that your family trust transfers money to him, and he funnels it to an offshore account," said Jasmin.

Jacob shook his head. "He's not being paid. That's part of his inheritance. He's a Perry. The bastard child of our father and some local nobody he had a one-night fling with. In exchange for not coming forth, he gets a stipend from the trust."

Torie and Jasmin stared at one another, mouth agape.

"You're the one who sent Emily the flash drive, aren't you? That's what you meant by helping her," said Torie. "You wanted her to have some leverage in fighting off the business development deal. She just never got a chance to use it."

Jacob said nothing, but he also couldn't meet her gaze any longer.

"So, we already know that if Samantha had gone through with her plans to terminate the development here, your family might be over extended...possibly bankrupt. How would that have impacted the sheriff?"

"Well, he wouldn't be getting those fat direct deposits anymore, that's for sure," replied Jacob.

"Jeez," said Jasmin. "Is there anyone in this town who didn't have motive to kill that woman?"

Chapter Fifteen

The conversation with Jacob had revealed far more than they had expected. He hadn't known anything about Samantha's plans, or what had caused her to pull out of supporting the development deal for the town. But he had confirmed that doing so would have, for the most part, been a debilitating blow for the company.

"The more I think about this, the more I feel like someone in her own family killed that woman," said Jasmin.

Torie nodded. "And for what? Money."

"No. The fear of losing money."

"I think that at the rate things are going, we are going to need something to help keep all these suspects straight," said Torie.

"Oh, like a murder Kanban," said Jasmin, laughing. "I do love a good Kanban."

Torie looked at her watch. "We have just enough time to shower and change, maybe a quick power nap. Did you speak with Kitty about the dinner tonight?"

"I did. We are all set."

"Okay, then. I'll see you in a couple of hours."

Torie retired to her room, thankful for a bit of downtime. This vacation turned murder mystery was not something she had expected and was completely outside her comfort zone. But she wholeheartedly believed in what they were doing. In the short time she had been there, she had taken a liking to the small town, and to some of the people.

In Emily, she sensed a kindred spirit; not magically, but on a deep, personal level. She liked the woman, and every instinct in her body told her that Emily was not a killer and had been singled out to take the fall for this heinous act.

Armed with new information, Torie desperately wished she could speak with Emily again. If only Sheriff Odette hadn't interrupted their conversation. She thought briefly about asking the sheriff to let her see the woman again, but then remembered his stern statement that Emily would not be available for questioning for forty-eight hours.

That was how long it would take to get the blood and DNA matching back, along with the analysis of the contents of the container from Emily's shop.

That didn't leave a lot of time to sift through the ever-growing list of suspects and find out who really killed Samantha.

Magic would make this all so much easier. But she heeded Jasmin's warning. These were humans, not supernaturals. Who knew what effect spells could have on them?

Rather than dwell on the subject, she cleared her mind and made her way over to a small writing desk against the far wall of her suite. There was a small pad and pencil on top which she picked up and started to organize her thoughts.

She was only half joking about a murder board and decided the best way to keep everything organized was to write down her suspicions, each tied to the possible suspect that raised them. Looking at her notes, she knew there was one thing missing, and it stood out like a sore thumb to her.

Alibis.

That was the one thing she had learned from watching untold hours of *Castle* and a multitude of other cop shows. You were supposed to ask each suspect where they were at the time of the murder and see if anyone could corroborate their story.

How could she have forgotten that? They would have to correct that tonight with Cameron. The thought of questioning the young man made her stomach twist in knots. She was worried that asking him for an alibi would immediately make him think she saw him as someone capable of committing murder, which she did not.

Still, it was a conversation that needed to happen. She decided to step into Torie's suite to discuss who wanted to take the lead in questioning Cameron. She was probably more tactful in her approach, but Jasmin was clearly crushing hard on the man. Even though she didn't stand a chance with him, he might find that charming enough to lower his guard.

It would be classic good cop, bad cop, and Torie relished the thought of playing the role of the hard-hitting, no-nonsense detective. She was finding that it was good to sometimes step out of one's comfort zone.

She sat down her pad and pushed back from the table as she stood. That was when it hit her.

The room began to swirl and had the table not been there to support her, she might have dropped to the floor. Her vision was blurry, and her head suddenly began to pound. She reached up, wiping the sweat from her brow as a bout of coughing racked her, threatening to squeeze the oxygen from her lungs.

There was a smell in the air that she wasn't familiar with, one that made her eyes water and her throat threaten to close. Looking up through cloudy eyes, she could just make out a mist pouring into her room through the ventilation system. Holding one hand over her mouth and nose, she staggered for the door.

The knob was cold in her clammy hand, and try as she might, she could not turn it. Someone had locked her in.

Someone was trying to kill her.

She slumped against the door, weakened, unable to call for help. She felt the room closing in on her as she looked around desperately for help. The door to the balcony was closed as well, and as the room started to darken, she knew she would never make it to it in time.

The panic welling inside her suddenly faded, replaced by anger. This was not her time to die. She had survived angry hedge witches, been attacked by vampires and creatures that most humans would never dream existed. All of them had tried multiple times to kill her, yet she was still standing.

There was no way she was going to be taken out by some mysterious vapors.

Her eyes glowed as she reached deep within herself, finding the spark of her magic and drawing it into her hand in the form of a ball of glowing energy that she sent screaming at the French doors leading to the balcony.

The glass and wood shattered, flying outward and covering the tiny stone landing. Once the space was opened. Torie raised both hands into the air, swirling them about her head in a complex pattern that drew the gas into an invisible globe before being funneled out the broken door and into the open air.

Finally able to breathe, Torie gasped a lungful of air as she dropped her hands to her knees to support her weight. A thought struck her, snapping her upright.

Jasmin.

Rushing to the door that joined their suites, she tried to open it, only to find it wouldn't budge. She shoved her magic into the lock on, blowing the knob free of the wood as she ran out of her room and into to her friend's.

"Jasmin!" she called, looking about frantically.

The sound of running water came from the en-suite, and she burst into the room, holding her breath as she realized the same deadly mass had filled the bathroom. She saw Jasmin, lying in the bathtub, the water still running, overflowing the tub around the unconscious witch.

"No!" Torie yelled, as she lifted both hands into the air, calling on her most primal magic.

Fire.

Enchanted flames rose all around her, licking at the vapors swirling in the air, burning them away in a shower of bright, orange sparks. Once the air was cleansed, Torie rushed to her friend, placing two fingers against the side of Jasmin's neck.

Her pulse was strong, and Torie breathed a sigh of relief as she splashed water up onto Jasmin's face, gently shaking her friend's shoulders to rouse her back to consciousness.

Jasmin stuttered, slowly blinking away the fog as she lifted her head, focusing on the face in front of her.

"Torie? What is going on?" She lifted her arms out of the water, looking at the overflowing mess as Torie turned the water off. "What happened? I must have fallen asleep."

Torie shook her head. "You didn't fall asleep. Someone gassed us. They just tried to kill us."

Just then, footsteps were heard running through the main part of the suite, followed by Sheriff Odette and Brad Henry rushing into the bathroom. The two men looked around and quickly turned their backs as they realized Jasmin was still in a state of undress.

"What is going on?" demanded the sheriff, calling over his shoulder. "The fire alarms for this room suddenly went off, and your neighbors in the next room said they heard shouting and crashing."

Torie looked up angrily. "Someone just tried to kill us is what's going on." She helped Jasmin out of the tub, steadying her as she wrapped her bathrobe around her wet body.

"What?" said Sheriff Odette, spinning around. "Why? How?"

"What are you doing here?" asked Jasmin, her voice ragged.

"Oh, I just happened to have stopped by for some coffee this morning and to check in on the Henrys. Looks like it's a good thing I did," he replied, leveling the two women with a look.

"Yeah. How lucky for us," said Torie, giving the officer a steely gaze.

"I've checked and rechecked the HVAC systems," said Brad Henry. "I don't see where the ventilation system was tampered with to do what the two of you experienced." He was shaking his head in dismay as he addressed the sheriff and the two women.

They were all gathered around the main table in the large kitchen. Penny was practically distraught over what had happened and had made a pot of tea and brought out a bottle of peach brandy, which she said was perfect for calming the nerves, and placed it on the table in front of Torie and Jasmin.

"You poor, poor girls," she said, one hand clasping the side of her cheek. "I can't imagine what must be going through your heads after having gone through that."

"Well, I'm just glad Torie was able to break that window to let the gas out and then save me," said Jasmin. "Otherwise, who knows how this could have ended."

"Uh huh," said Sheriff Odette. "Now, about that, can you tell me again, just what happened?" He had his notepad and tiny pencil at the ready.

"Well, sir, as I said, I was in my suite minding my business, when I was overcome by some very powerful and noxious fumes. I really thought I was going to die; everything was spinning and going black. As luck would have it, I was able to break the glass on the door and the breeze outside drew out the fumes enough for me to get out.

"Knowing that Jasmin and I had adjoining suites, I went to check on her and found her bathroom so covered in a layer of the fumes that I couldn't really see her. I had a lighter in my pocket and held it up, which must have interacted in some way with the gas to burn it off. That's when I saw her passed out in the tub. You know what happened from there."

He was nodding slowly as his eyes trailed down the line of notes he had previously written. "Yes. And, what happened with the doorknobs? And what did you use to break the glass on the door in your suite?"

Torie looked about, confused. "I'm not sure. It all

happened so fast. Maybe I just don't know my own strength." She gave him another hard look, refusing to break the stare he returned.

"Alright, that's enough of that, Ben Odette," scolded Penny. "You stop with this interrogation right now. These women have been through an ordeal, they don't need your harassment adding to their horrible experience. Let's just be thankful everyone is okay."

Finally, the sheriff looked away, shoving his notepad back into his pocket before turning his attention to the Henrys.

"I guess you're right. It is a good thing no one else has been hurt on your property. I can't imagine how that would play out. I'm betting you're both pretty glad you decided to sell this place; before any more…incidents occur."

He pushed back from the table, tipping his hat at everyone in the room as he turned to walk away.

"I'm going to go write this up as an accident," he said, not turning to look at anyone. "If you think of anything else, let me know. You can find me at the jailhouse; I'll be there for quite a while. Doing paperwork."

Torie couldn't help but flinch as his last couple of words struck her. She was certain he would be on high alert now, so no more chances to sneak into the cell and visit Emily.

A knock on the door frame caught everyone's attention, and they turned to see Cameron standing in the entryway.

His features clouded over with concern as he felt the tension in the room.

"Oh no," he said, looking at everyone. "Did someone else die?"

Jasmin coughed, gathering her robe closer about her body and looking away from the young man.

"Just my dignity," she said, giving Torie a horrified look.

Chapter Sixteen

"You know, I completely understand if you want to cancel. I mean, yeah, this place is renowned for its venison tenderloin, and I was really looking forward to it; but you two almost died."

Torie, Jasmin and Cameron sat inside the large sunroom on the back of the inn, waiting for the signal that their dinner was ready. The large coffee table before them was set with two beautiful charcuterie boards and a bottle of Cabernet. Kitty had filled each glass, giving the women an extra pour on account of the day they had, and had promised to call them when their main meal was ready. Even though they insisted everything would be okay, Brad had closed the upper terrace near their rooms until he could have someone come and check the large HVAC system that was hidden from view at the back of the upper terrace.

"What I'm trying to say is that I would completely understand a rain check," said Cameron. "I mean, shouldn't you be resting?"

Torie smiled at the young man. "Thank you for the offer, but that won't be necessary."

"If we rested every time someone tried to kill us, we would never get off the couch," said Jasmin, waving her hand dismissively and adding her smile to Torie's.

Cameron frowned, not quite sure how to take her words.

"Don't pay any attention to her," Torie said. "She's still high from the gases. But no, rescheduling won't be necessary." She took a deep breath and cleared her throat. "After everything that's happened, there is just no easy way to do this, so I'm just going to jump right in. Cameron, we asked you here for a very specific reason. I'm embarrassed to ask this but—"

Cameron held up a hand before she could finish the sentence.

"Ladies. I'm really very flattered, but I have to tell you that I'm very happily married. And gay."

Torie could feel the scarlet creeping up her neck as she and Jasmin stared at him.

"Oh, I think we have given you the wrong idea. We weren't about to ask you...that," said Torie.

Jasmine chuckled, shaking her head. "Child, I would break you," she mumbled.

Torie ignored her friend and kept talking. "No, Cameron, what we wanted to ask is, where were you the morning Samantha Perry was killed?"

He looked at the women in shock, his brows slowly knitting together as he realized what they were asking.

"I was home. With my husband. I was running late to open the shop that morning because we had an argument the night before. That morning I wanted to make sure everything was okay between us, so we were discussing some issues in more depth." He swallowed, reaching for his wine glass. "Feel free to check with him, as to the time I left. I had nothing to do with Mrs. Perry's murder."

Just then, Kitty approached the group, hands clasped in front of her.

"Ladies. Gentlemen. Your meal is ready. This way please."

She led them through the sunroom and onto the back terrace where a large, round table had been set with bone china dinnerware and gorgeous Waterford wine glasses. Silver flatware against a white tablecloth finished off the table set, all of which was impeccably lit by an array of candles adding just the right amount of glow.

"Oh, Kitty, it's beautiful," said Torie. "Thank you so much."

Once they were seated, Kitty left to bring their wine and the meal.

Torie turned her attention back to the young man at the table.

"Cameron, we know you didn't have anything to do with it, but we have to ask. We're trying to help prove that Emily is innocent and to do that we have to rule out everyone who had potential motive to hurt Samantha."

"What makes you think I have motive?" he replied.

"We heard that the Perrys were putting the squeeze on your supply chain. That your store was suffering as a result and was about to go under," said Jasmin.

The smell of perfectly roasted venison invaded their senses as Kitty pushed a gold trolley up to the table. There was a large tenderloin on display, which she expertly carved into three pieces and placed on the plates before them. To accompany the tenderloin, she heaped aromatic steamed apples and baby potatoes that glistened in black truffle oil and fresh herbs.

She then carefully spooned the perfect amount of a dark, plum-colored reduction over the meat, leaving a small bowl of the sauce in the center of the table for them in case they wanted more.

"That's a port and fig reduction that I think you'll really like," she said. She then checked that they were still good with the amount of wine left in the bottle, before removing the trolley and leaving them to their conversation.

"I'm sorry if I came across as defensive. You're right to ask. I want to try and help Emily as much as possible. Everyone in town does. We all know she didn't do it," Cameron said.

"Thank you for saying that. And you don't have to be sorry for anything. We were the ones who were so worried about asking you this. Right, Jasmin?"

A moan was all that escaped Jasmin's lips, and the two other dinner guests turned to see her biting into a sizable piece of the venison smeared with the port reduction. Her eyes were closed, and she looked like she had been transported to another, more blissful, realm.

"I'm sorry, what did you ask?" she said, eyes snapping open as she realized someone was speaking to her. "Cos this is heavenly, and I am experiencing things."

They all laughed, the tension leaving the air as they enjoyed the amazing meal and drink. Kitty appeared again, at just the perfect moment, to remove the dishes.

"And for dessert, we have Bananas Foster, prepared tableside for you, along with our homemade vanilla bean ice cream. Would you be interested in trying some?"

"Girl, you had me at homemade vanilla bean. Bring it on," said Jasmin.

They made small talk, and Torie took out her phone to record Kitty as she returned and went about creating the rich dessert for them. There were "oohs" and "aahs" as the flames licked at the evening light, burning off the rum.

"That was...incredible," said Cameron as the evening wore down.

"Well, we just wanted to thank you for being so welcoming to us," said Torie.

"And to pay you back for all those free coffees," added Jasmin.

"And don't forget to interrogate me as well," Cameron said, flashing his smile. "Just kidding. No offense taken."

They all excused themselves from the table and made their way through the inn to the front door, where Cameron stretched, patting his stomach in content.

"That might be the best meal I've ever had. Just don't tell the hubby I said that. Speaking of which, his number. Feel free to call him to confirm my timeline." He took one of the fliers from the entry table and scribbled a number on the back before handing it over to Torie. "And if you need help with anything involving all of this, please don't hesitate to reach out to me. Hopefully I see you tomorrow for coffee."

With that, he headed for his car, waving back at them, before easing out of the drive and out of sight.

"Well, we can cross that one off the list," said Torie.

"And that's a relief. He's a good man, most of the people in this town are."

All except one, Torie thought to herself. And we need to find them.

"Well, I'm off to bed. I'm way too stuffed to stay up any longer," said Jasmin.

They said their good nights and headed up the stairs to

their rooms. Brad had offered repeatedly to move them, but they had declined, opting to stay where they were once the smashed doors and glass had been cleaned. What was the likelihood there would be a second accident that could result in their deaths? Torie had reasoned with him. Jasmin had told her later that since they both knew it wasn't an accident, the likelihood was actually quite high.

That was when they both decided to set up wards inside the room. A simple protection spell had been said to activate upon their entry, and it would also let them know if someone had entered their space while they were away.

Crossing the room, Torie headed for her small balcony, relishing the feel of the cool night air on her skin as she stood outside, breathing deeply. She looked up at the moon. The fullness of it illuminated the landscape below her. For a moment, she felt her mind focus on her werewolf boyfriend, and she considered calling him just to check in. But she also knew that if she did that, he would sense something amiss and would be able to get out of her what was going on.

Once that happened, she knew there would be no way to stop him from coming to The Sweetbriar to be at her side. Though she liked to pretend otherwise, his protective side always made her smile. He truly was her knight in shining fur.

Movement below caught her eye. A shape moved from the edge of the bushes to the stairs that led up to the terrace. It headed for the side of the patio that was covered in shadows. The area where the locked door leading to the catacombs were.

Who would be out there this time of night?

Something about the way the figure moved made her think of the night she had seen Samantha with someone on the terrace in that same spot. As part of their questioning,

Jacob had denied being with her that last night of her life, so maybe, whoever was down there was the last person to see Samantha alive.

She turned and headed out of her suite, making her way to Jasmin's. She raised her hand to knock, but then remembered how tired her friend was and thought better of disturbing her. After all, it was probably nothing. And it wasn't like she couldn't take care of herself.

Turning, she headed down the stairs, taking them as quickly as she could, and made her way through the back of the inn to the French doors that led to the terrace. Once outside, she quickly headed for the side, stepping from the pale light of the moon into the darkness of shadow.

Her eyes adjusted enough that she could make out the door built into the side of the stone. She gave the handle a tug, and sure enough, the door swung open with a rusty whine. She peered inside at total blackness, remembering what Brad had told her about there being no power to the lights down there any longer.

The hair on the back of her neck stood up and goose-bumps raced down her arms as she took a tentative step into the dark enclosure. Taking a deep breath, she summoned a small ball of light to illuminate just the area in front of her. There were stone steps carved into the earth that led down-ward, the stairwell so tight she felt the beginning of claus-trophobia closing in on her.

Shaking off the crushing feeling, she took her first steps down, part of her thinking that maybe she should have woken Jasmin.

Chapter Seventeen

Picking her way carefully down the stairs, the first thing that struck Torie was the overwhelming smell of packed earth. The stairs led to a well-worn dirt path that looked like it may have been heavily travelled at one point. It was tight at first, but then opened so it was wide enough that two medium-sized adults could have probably walked side by side through it, with the ceiling height being just above her head.

There were old light fixtures protruding from the stone walls every few yards, but none of them were lit. The only light came from the glowing ball that hovered over her shoulder as she made her way forward.

The air, while smelling of dirt, should have been stale if this passageway was sealed up for as long as Brad claimed. Yet she could make out the faintest touch of a breeze blowing at her back. Something was circulating fresh air through the space. She fought the urge to sneeze as she crept forward, following a straight path for what felt like a few hundred yards before she came to a fork.

"Great. Which one?"

She mulled her two decisions over, also acutely aware of the fact that if there were any more deviations in the path, she could very well get lost down here. That wouldn't do. Who would even know to come looking for her down here if that happened?

She stooped down to examine the path. To the left, the dirt seemed undisturbed; but there were slight footprints to the one that veered to the right. Whoever she was following had gone that way, so it made sense for her to do so as well.

Unless of course it was the killer. Somehow, she didn't think they would take kindly to being followed.

Taking a breath, she pressed forward, heading down the right passageway. The fact that it closed in slightly didn't make her feel any better. There were roots and dried vines starting to poke through the ceiling, dropping down into her face, tickling the back of her head as she moved beneath them.

Just when she thought it might be time to head back, she felt the breeze pick up, this time coming from in front of her. There was also the scent of fresh fruit and leaves in the air, letting her know there had to be an opening to the outside.

Sure enough, the passageway widened until she was standing at an opening ringed with roots and vegetation. Extinguishing the glow of her magic, she pushed through the wet, clinging vines and made her way out of the tunnel to face an embankment of mud and slippery stones.

The wet earth and stone chilled her hands to the bone as she pulled her way up the embankment, clawing to the top of what was once a riverbed. Had the tunnels been formed by flowing water originally? That could explain why they were so crudely cut into the landscape.

As she crested the top of the hill from where she had emerged, she looked back and could barely make out the entrance to the tunnel. It was perfectly concealed in the overgrowth that grew down the side of the bank. Had she not known it was there, she might have walked right by it without giving it a second look.

Her cold hands rested on her knees as she took in the air to soothe her burning lungs. She also took the opportunity to rub her aching knees as the joints protested loudly against the labor she had just put them through.

Looking around, there was something familiar about the area she was standing in, but she wasn't sure why. The moonlight played tricks with her vision; casting shadow where there would be none during the day, illuminating areas differently from how her eyes might normally perceive them.

Drawing herself upright, she made her way forward, her senses coming alive to every nuance around her. The crack of a branch caught her attention, and she slowly followed the sound until she could make out a voice floating on the night breeze.

Torie made her way around a large group of trees, and that was when she realized where she was. There was a small clearing ahead of her, and in that clearing was a group of stones that surrounded the mineral pool where she and Jasmin had bathed earlier.

The same pool where Samantha Perry had been killed.

On the other side of the pool were woods that bordered the back of The Sweetbriar, the ones she and Jasmin had crossed through to get to the hot spring. The tunnel route she had taken had been considerably quicker, albeit scarier, than the trek through the scenic woods. But if she had gotten to the pool so quickly, then that meant the killer could have gotten there and out just in the same, or less, amount of time.

Again, she heard a faint voice and ducked back behind the tree, only poking her head out just enough to see the waterline of the hot spring. As her eyes adjusted to the light, she could just make out the figure of the person she had seen on the terrace standing next to the water.

He was speaking with someone. Someone standing just outside her field of view. The man's voice was deep but animated, and she could only make out certain words, but she was sure she made out the phrase "should be dead".

There was a pause before the man spoke again. Whoever he was talking to was speaking so softly that Torie could not hear their words at all.

She needed a closer look.

Creeping around the far side of the tree, she stuck to the shadows and made her way closer, moving from the cover of one large tree to the next, careful to avoid the moonlight that broke between the branches. Finally, she had managed to make her way around the foliage until she was closer to the mineral pool and the shadowy figure as well.

The man had his back to her and was nodding vigorously to someone, a few grunts punctuating the air at intervals. Leaning around the other side of the tree from which she was hiding, Torie could finally make out who he was speaking to.

Or rather, *what* he was speaking to.

Despite herself, she gasped audibly at the spectral figure that floated just a few inches off the ground in front of the man.

While it was clearly translucent, the outline formed by the creature was not that of a human. It had the vague outline of humanoid features, but there were no limbs or head that she could make out. During her time as a hex witch, she had seen more than her fair share of ghosts—including that of her own mother—and they had always appeared in death just as they had in life; the only exception being that they were practically see through.

This thing, however, was different. Whatever it had been in life, it wasn't a human being.

Her gasp alerted the two to her presence. The man immediately broke off and ran into the woods that led to the back of the inn, while the ghastly apparition turned its attention to Torie, becoming less translucent as it floated in her direction.

Torie felt an overwhelming sense of anger emanating from the creature as it moved towards her. The air between them practically shivered with rage.

Torie called up her magic, channeling it into her hand as she held up her arms, the blue energy swirling around them.

The creature slowed its advance, clearly not expecting the response she had presented.

"Stop right there," Torie said, trying to steady her voice as much as possible. "If you can understand me, I don't mean you any harm, but you should know that I can and will defend myself."

The creature hesitated, black light beginning to spark within its ghostly frame, fireworks trapped within a patch of dark sky.

Torie looked past the apparition only to see that the human who had been conversing with it had disappeared into the night. She returned her attention to the business at hand, circling slowly, hands pulsing with power.

In response, the creature increased its own glow, the patterns of lights increasing in speed and size. Torie watched, unsure if the creature meant to attack, even though it had stopped advancing on her. With that thought in mind, she swallowed back her fear and slowly recalled her magic, reducing her power until her fists no longer glowed blue.

To her relief, the creature did the same, the light show inside its amorphous body dissipating until she faced only a vague, gray outline hovering before her.

She took a step back, and the creature took a step forward. She stopped moving, and it stopped moving. It was as if they were locked in a macabre, scary, two step. A supernatural box step and neither of them knew who was leading.

The creature slowly moved backwards, floating in the air and then stopping. Torie followed, covering the same distance forward as the apparition had retreated. Torie waited, nodding slowly. She hadn't been threatened, if anything the fact that it had just been communicating with someone else put her a little more at ease.

She watched as it moved slowly back and to the side until it was hovering over the mineral pool.

Now what? She bit her lower lip as she stepped towards the pool, tentatively approaching the edge.

The creature began to pulse lightly, tiny pieces of itself seemed to break away and float down to the surface of the pool, illuminating the water in shimmering shades of green and yellow.

"You want me to get into the water?" asked Torie.

The creature pulsed lightly and again showered the pond with strobes of light. Torie could see tiny vapors of steam rising from the pool as she bent down to remove her shoes to slip one foot into the water, just to see what effect it would have on the creature.

Just as she was about to dip in her toe, Jasmin's voice rang out from the other side of the pond.

"Torie, stop!"

"Jasmin? What are you doing out here?" Torie said, her foot hovering in midair.

"Torie, step back from that thing. Trust me."

She didn't even question what her friend was saying as she immediately jumped back away from the water. She watched as Jasmin reached the edge of the pond, extending both her arms in front of her as her magic shimmered in the night air, casting a dome of blue over the pond and the apparition hovering above it.

"Help me!" she said to Torie. "We need to contain this thing before—"

Before Torie could reach out and add her magic to her friend's, the ghostly shape dissolved into a mass of light, sinking into the water before disappearing completely from view.

Jasmin dropped her magic and rushed to Torie's side.

"Are you okay?" she asked.

"I'm fine," Torie said, staring at the now still waters. "I think that thing was trying to communicate with me. I was thinking it might know something about Samantha's murder."

Jasmin's eyes grew big as she pointed at the spring. "That thing can't tell you anything. That was a siphon, a construct designed to steal and trap the essence of a living being. I could feel the magic it was giving off from my room. It actually woke me from my sleep. When I felt your magic flare to life, I knew you were probably doing something ill advised, like trying to communicate with it." She shook her head, looking from Torie to the pond and back to

Torie again. "Do you know what would have happened had it lured you into that water?"

Torie shuddered. She was incredibly fond of her life essence and didn't like the idea of forcibly being made to part ways with it.

"Torie, this type of siphon isn't easy to create or control. Did you see the person who made it?"

"I saw someone…I followed them through the tunnel from the terrace. It ran underground and came out here. But when they became aware of my presence, they took off…leaving that thing behind. I thought it was running the show."

Jasmin shook her head.

"Not at all. Whoever you saw, is collecting souls. Looks like our killer is tied to the supernatural. Things in this sleepy little town just got a heck of a lot more interesting."

Chapter Eighteen

The next morning, Torie sat in her bath, brushing her hair and staring into the mirror. Despite their best efforts, she and Jasmin had not been able to track down where the person she saw had disappeared to. Whomever it was, they had cloaked their trail with some pretty sophisticated magic that thwarted even their hex spells.

They even tried a reversal spell to see if it was possible to bring the siphon back, but to no avail. Whatever they were now facing was very adept at evade and capture. Still, knowing what they might be up against, leveled the playing field a bit. After all, magic was their specialty, and they were betting that whoever was behind this, had no idea just what the two of them were capable of.

At least that was the hope.

Jasmin had assured her that anyone capable of creating a siphon like the one she had witnessed was not going to be a pushover, even with their combined power.

"Is it another witch?" Torie had asked.

"Not necessarily. That's the thing about magic, you

don't have to be a witch to gain a semblance of control over it. It's like being a chef. It can take all of their skill to create a delicate consommé that is beyond our abilities to make; but they can also use their skills to make a cheese omelet, which anyone can learn to do."

The fact that her magical abilities had been compared to omelet making didn't fill Torie with confidence, but it did add a new layer of paranoia when it came to looking for potential suspects. Now, they were not only looking for a human killer, but also one that was possibly versed in the art of magic.

She wished she had her library back at her house to peruse. Her mother had been a powerful witch in her own right and had gathered a considerable number of tomes on the subject. Surely there would be something in one of those books that mentioned siphons and how to deal with them.

For her part, Jasmin's knowledge was limited on the subject, though she did tell Torie how to recognize the particular hum of magic that was created with the sole purpose of trapping energy. It felt like a tickle on the roof of one's mouth.

The way she described it made Torie think of the Pop Rocks she used to love as a child. At least until her mother told her that some child somewhere in some country had swallowed a mouthful of Pop Rocks and then immediately drank a soda and their stomach exploded.

Even though she was certain it never happened, Torie never ate another Rock after hearing that story. Even now, she shuddered at the thought and pushed the mental imagery to the back of her mind.

The addition of magic into an already horrific crime added another element that made her uneasy. If a human had somehow managed to utilize arcane power to kill—not just kill but enslave a being's soul—then they had to be stopped. No matter the cost. This was something she and Jasmin had done before, and she knew from experience that it would not end well.

The thought of harming any creature never sat well with her, but it was especially troubling when it came to using her powers against a human. But this particular human had shown them they weren't helpless, and what's more, were particularly vicious. Who knew how many people had been hurt over time.

She stopped brushing her hair mid-stroke as that thought hit her. Slamming down her brush, she rushed from her suite to Jasmin's locked door. A few fast raps of her knuckles, and her friend flung open the door.

"What is it? Are you okay?" Jasmin asked.

"I'm fine. But I had a thought." She brushed past her friend to enter the room, closing the door behind her. "What's the likelihood that this is the first time whoever is behind this has killed someone?"

Jasmin frowned. "Probably not likely. Where is this coming from?"

"Well, I'm just thinking back to that creature—the siphon—from last night. You said that it was constructed to collect the essence of living beings, right? Well, do you think all those twinkling lights inside it were those collections? The souls of everyone it's harvested?"

"I don't know. That thing was lit up like a Christmas tree. That would mean this has been going on for a very long time."

"And is that out of the realm of possibility? You said yourself you don't know how this thing works."

Jasmin nodded her head. "You're right. But how do we

even proceed with finding more out about it? It hides from our magic."

Torie considered her friend's words. "True, but maybe there is another way. I'm betting the human who controls it doesn't rely on magic for everything. Get dressed. I have an idea."

An hour later, they were parking their bikes outside the town library. It was a beautiful old Victorian that had been converted in the seventies. It sat a couple of blocks back from Main Street, with only a couple of cars sitting in the gravel parking lot. Walking inside, they were hit with one of Torie's favorite smells; old books.

"So, what exactly are we doing here?" asked Jasmin as they approached the main desk, looking for a librarian.

There was a handwritten note on the counter that read, "Restocking, please ring bell for service". Torie did as the sign requested, gently dinging a small silver bell that sat beside the piece of paper.

"Well, we can't exactly waltz into the sheriff's office and ask to see the town's police records on any murders dating back for the last ten to twenty years. Can you imagine what he would do? But every small town has a public record of newsworthy events. I'm betting even Sheriff Odette can't purge those files; if he has something to do with all of this, that is."

"That's a big leap," said Jasmin. "We still don't know that he is involved. I mean, yes, he is collecting money from the Perrys, but it's money he's entitled to. That doesn't make him a killer."

"I didn't say it did," said Torie. "But he is definitely

trying to cover this crime up, or at the very least, he's fine sending the wrong person to jail in an effort to sweep this under the rug. Either way, he's not going to be very forthcoming in helping us get to the bottom of what is really going on around here. We can at least see if there is any history of something like this happening before."

They both turned to greet the young man who appeared from behind one of the rows of bookshelves, pushing a trolley laden with all manner of books. He looked to be around thirty and gave them a cursory smile as he wheeled the cart behind the desk and out of view.

"Hello ladies, how may I help you today?" he asked. His smile was dazzling and seemed to come naturally to him.

His warmth made Torie like him immediately.

"We need to look through your local paper archives. I assume you have that here?" she said.

He nodded, raising a pair of glasses hanging from a silver chain around his neck. "I do indeed. Are you members of the library?"

Both women shook their head.

"I'm afraid not. We aren't locals," Jasmin said. "We were passing through and our car broke down, so we're kind of stuck here for a bit. We just find this place so intriguing and beautiful that we wanted to learn a little more about your history."

The man stared at them, his hazel eyes blinking and then growing wide.

"Holy crap! Are you Torie and Jasmin?" he asked, trying to contain his obvious excitement.

The women looked at one another, not quite sure how to take the younger man. He clasped his hands in front of him, his smile widening.

"Well, I guess our reputation precedes us," said Jasmin, forcing a nervous smile of her own.

"I am Michael," he said. "Cameron's husband. He told me all about you ladies. He said you are trying to clear poor Emily's name."

The tension flowed out of Torie and Jasmin as they each shook his hand. He was not much taller than they were, yet they could tell he was powerfully built. The sleeves of his button-up shirt strained to contain his arms as he pumped their hands.

"I have to say, I was starting to doubt the two of you existed. But here you are. In my library. I can't believe it. Though I have to say I am a bit annoyed that Cameron came home regaling me with tales of the fabulous meal you treated him to. Don't get me wrong, I don't mean to imply that I wish I was there, but the very least Cameron could have done would be to bring me a tiny piece of that succulent venison he raved about."

He dropped his hands, clasping them in front of him. Torie saw a shadow pass across his features, and for a moment she thought he was going to break into a pout. But instead, he just waved his hands over his head, dismissing whatever it was that had momentarily flitted through him.

"But that's not a big deal. I just made him promise to take me to The Sweetbriar for dinner one evening and he better not complain once about the cost." Again, he shook his head, smiling good-naturedly at them. "But listen to me prattling on about fancy food. That's not what you are here for. You're looking for something. A clue perhaps that will help you discover who the real killer is? Is that why you want to see our archives?"

Torie nodded slowly, her mind racing to keep up with the young man.

"Yes, something like that," she answered. "We need to know if there have been other deaths in town that were unexplained."

"Or not investigated properly," said Michael, nodding and giving Torie a wink. "I gotcha. Follow me."

He led them to a private room off the main floor of the library. The door leading to it was marked 'research' and contained five small cubicles, each with a computer and a microfiche reader.

"I haven't seen one of these in decades," said Torie. "It's a shame to admit that's how long it's been since I was in a library."

Michael gave her a disapproving look. "Yeah, maybe don't admit that to people. Civilizations were built on the backs of libraries. It still bothers me what happened in Alexandria..." His voice trailed off wistfully until he realized the two women were staring at him. "What? I just feel like if I had been there, I could have done something."

This caused both Torie and Jasmin to break out into smiles. Michael laughed at himself and ushered them both to a cubicle next to a window, overlooking the back of the building. He brought an extra chair from an adjoining cube for them, but before leaving the room, he turned to the women.

"So, are you going to ask me?"

"Ask you what?" answered Jasmin.

"About Cameron's alibi. He didn't tell me what you discussed with him over dinner, but I've seen enough television shows that I'm sure it came up."

Torie's smile faded, and she could feel heat rising in her neck. "I am really sorry we had to do that. But we needed to cross him off the list."

Michael was shaking his head. "Don't be sorry. Truth is,

neither of us are fond of the Perrys. They have highly questionable business tactics. But we were together that morning. Plus, neither of us have a strong stomach when it comes to violence." He closed his eyes, shivering at the thought.

"So, how does all this work?" asked Torie, indicating the research equipment before her.

"Well, the computers are local only, they don't scour the internet, but they do link to every newspaper article in the tri-county area over the last twenty-five years. All searchable just as you would any database. If you're looking for something beyond that, then you'll need to use the micro readers. All of that information is stored on microfilm that I can help you pull. Just yell when you need something."

With that, he was gone, whistling happily to himself as he made his way back to the front of the library.

"Man, talk about having it all. Just when I thought Cameron couldn't get any hotter, he gets to go home to that every night," Jasmin said. "Okay, let's fire this bad boy up and see what we can find."

Torie flicked on the computer and, after some careful consideration, typed a few words into the search bar.

Ten minutes later, the two of them sat in dumbfounded silence staring at the screen.

"Holy crap," Torie said. "This town has to be the murder capital of the free world. And no one has ever said a word about it."

Chapter Nineteen

"Well, if it's not the murder capital, it's certainly up there," said Jasmin.

They stared at the computer screen, not quite sure what the numbers they were seeing meant. The first search they had tried had not returned much in the way of murders in the town or the surrounding counties. But then, they removed the filter for residents living in the town or county, and the numbers showed a completely different story.

"There are less than five thousand people living in this town. Maybe seventy-five thousand in these four counties put together," said Torie, gesturing at the screen. "But over the last fifteen years there have been almost a thousand disappearances or deaths in the area...mostly all of them have been from out of town."

Jasmin had her phone out and was tapping quickly at the screen before looking up at Torie.

"Almost none of these have been reported outside of these vague clippings from this local newspaper. How is that possible?"

"And how is it possible that none of these have follow ups? It's almost like they were posted and then forgotten about," added Torie, scrolling through the articles.

"When was the most recent?" asked Jasmin.

Torie sorted the articles and began scrolling through the post.

"There is no mention of Samantha here, but it says there was a young woman named Dorothy Kline who was killed four years ago. Nothing since then."

"There are a rash of disappearances and murders for over a decade, then it just stopped, only to happen again a couple of days ago. Why is there no mention of Samantha Perry's death?" said Jasmin.

Torie tapped her finger nervously, trying to piece together the story of what they were seeing. Then she had an idea and furiously tapped out a search on the computer.

"Look at this." She pointed out articles as she scrolled through them. "In the beginning, these were full-fledged articles. Bios of the missing or murdered people that were meticulously researched. But as time goes by, the articles get progressively smaller, until they are little more than filler mentions. And another thing, they are all written by the same person."

Jasmin squinted at the screen. "James Keller. Wait, maybe he's local." Again, Jasmin's fingers played across her screen before she held it up triumphantly. "According to FriendBook, he does indeed live just on the outskirts of town. Looks like we are going to need young Mr. Michael's help after all."

Together, they made their way to the front desk where Michael was scanning barcodes on the spines of book jackets, humming along contentedly to whatever was playing in his earbuds. Torie cleared her throat, and finally knocked on the countertop to get the man's attention. He jumped at the sound before removing his earbuds and offering a smile.

"Oh geez, I forgot you were here. You didn't need to come all the way back up here. You should have just called out and I would have come running to you."

Torie and Jasmin exchanged looks and gave him the tiniest hint of a smile.

"Oh no, we feel like we've already been such an imposition on you, we couldn't have done that," said Torie. "However, there is a favor we'd like to ask. Do you know where this is?" She handed over Jasmin's phone and pointed to James Keller's bio on the social media platform that included pictures of his farm.

"Sure, that's old Mr. Keller. He lives off route 321. Not the nicest of people. What do you need him for?" His eyes lit up, widening. "Is he a suspect? He is, isn't he?"

"He's not a suspect," said Jasmin. "But he is someone we need to talk to. Is his place within biking distance?"

"Oh yeah. It's easy from here. I don't know the exact address or I'd put it in your phone. But you can't miss his farm."

Torie held up a hand. "Is it a bikeable distance...for the two of us?"

Michael deliberated a little too long, which gave Torie her answer. She spoke up, saving him from saying something he would have definitely regretted.

"I hate to ask, but do you have a car we could borrow? I wouldn't ask, but we really need to speak with him in person," Torie said.

"You know what? I'd be happy to drive you over," Michael said. "There has not been a soul in here all day 'cept for you two. No one will even notice if I close up for a bit."

"Oh no, we couldn't," said Jasmin. "We can't put you out like that."

He looked at them, reaching under the counter to fish out his keys and holding them up. "Fine. But can you drive a three-speed manual with the shifter on the column, old Chevy pickup? It's a custom job."

Torie looked at him, blinking. "I don't even know what you just said." She sighed, motioning for him to follow behind them. "Come on. Let's go."

The ride out to the Keller farm was bumpy and hot. There was no suspension to speak of on Michael's 'custom' pickup, and the air conditioning was limited to rolling down the two windows only halfway, because any further and they simply got stuck and would require gentle rocking with both hands while someone else worked the manual crank to get them back in place. Or at least that was how Michael put it.

Still, the ride through the countryside was beautiful. Once out of town, the vegetation on the hillsides grew wild with honeysuckle and white and lavender wildflowers taking over. Rolling hills covered in hay dotted the landscape, and Torie couldn't help but marvel at the raw beauty of the countryside.

"Michael, I thought you said this was within biking distance," Jasmin said.

"Oh, it is."

"For whom? Lance Armstrong?" she replied.

After a few more minutes, Michael made a right turn on an unmarked, gravel driveway. Tall grasses that came halfway up the truck lined either side of the drive as they made their way towards a simple, white clapboard house that appeared entirely unremarkable. There was an open shed to one side that acted as a garage, housing an old Jeep Wrangler. A picket fence encased the back yard of the house, running in both directions nearly as far as the eye could see. It was an impressive piece of land James Keller owned.

Michael's pickup groaned and coughed to a stop just before the shed-garage, and he creaked open the door so he could come around and do the same for the two ladies.

Not that they needed any reason to sneak up to the front door, but if they had, the crunch of gravel underfoot would have made that impossible. The porch was newly painted, and they could see signs that the windows and front door had recently been replaced as well. Flower boxes adorned the railing that spanned the length of the porch, and the smell of fresh potting soil greeted them.

Torie stepped up to the front door and knocked. The door gave way under her hand, easing open slightly. They all exchanged looks. This might be the kind of area where people left their doors unlocked but leaving them open was a completely different matter.

"Hello? Mr. Keller?" Torie called out. She knocked again on the door, this time a little harder, pushing it open just a bit more. That was when it hit her. The smell of magic, dark and foul.

"Michael, go back to the truck, and no matter what you think you hear or see, do not step into the house," said Jasmin. She practically pushed him off the porch as she and Torie rushed into the house. The air reeked with the smell of magic; it seeped from every corner of the main living area that opened up before them.

Torie closed her eyes, feeling through the stench that threatened to overpower her senses as she looked for the source of the darkness. When she opened her eyes, wispy gray tendrils, like gossamer threads, weaved their way across the floor, disappearing out the back of the room. They followed the threads through the kitchen until they ended at a closed door on the back wall.

Torie glanced at Jasmin, nodding her head, as they slowly made their way to the door. She could feel the pulsations of magic emanating from the other side. Whatever had caused such a dark disturbance was on the other side.

She glanced at her friend and saw that her eyes were glowing with yellow power. Torie reached deep. Pulling her own magic up so that it vibrated on the tip of her tongue. Whatever was on the other side of that door was not prepared for what the two of them could unleash.

What she wasn't prepared for was the horror that greeted them when she flung the door open. They stepped into a screened-in sunroom filled with light and decorated with comfortable, overstuffed chairs and a large, dining-sized outdoor table. Strewn across that table was the body of James Keller. At least they assumed it was him; but they also knew that nothing short of his dental records would be able to positively identify the man. His face was ashen gray and severely wrinkled and caved in. It reminded Torie of the awful depiction of island head shrinkers that were popular in movies from her childhood. The man was on his back and his head hung over the edge of the table, sallow eyes drawn so far back into their sockets that they were practically invisible, staring at the women.

His body was moving slightly, and had they not been so focused on the state of him, they might have noticed the ghastly form that rose up, straddling the dead man. It was opaque and gray, with flecks of black lights popping randomly inside its form.

It was the same creature Torie had met at the mineral pond. Only this time, it was far more sinister in its appearance and its shape was less globular and more defined. It was lean, with a torso too elongated compared to its lower body. It squatted on bowed legs that ended in hooves for feet, and long arms that seemed to bend at odd angles rested on the dead man's chest. The creature was leaning forward, a gaping maw, the only opening in what would have been its face, was inches from the body's chest. Wisps of gray smoke, not unlike the trails they had followed through the house, were coming from the dead man and pouring into the monster's toothless mouth.

Torie gasped, the sight of the creature drinking in the man's soul froze her in place.

"No!" screamed Jasmin, pushing past her friend. "*Attori née impass denir!*" She threw her hand outward in an arc at the same time she spoke her incantation, and a pulse of yellow power swept forth, striking the creature in the side. The beast shimmered where it was hit by her magic and looked up, zeroing in on them with eyeless senses. But then it returned to its feeding, almost as if their presence was of no concern to it whatsoever.

Again, Jasmin attacked. This time, she created a wall of magic that she tried to insert between the creature and the body he was feasting on. Again, it shrugged off her attack, breaking the glowing wall of power that attempted to interfere with his feeding. Jasmin grunted and held out her hands. Torie could feel the power she was drawing on and looked around the room. On the far side of the wall was another, smaller table. This one was covered with bags of potting soil and flowerpots. Beside one of the pots was a trowel, the blade covered in dirt.

Torie held out her hand, using her magic to call the tiny

shovel to her. When it appeared in her palm, she levitated it in the air before them.

"Now!" she said to her friend.

Jasmin released her power in a bolt of magic that turned the trowel into a mini missile, sending it screaming across the room towards the creature. The impact drove it into the monster's side, lodging it inside the creature where the pops of light bounced off it, spraying sparks in all directions inside the beast.

The siphon reared its head back and howled. For the first time, it stopped its feeding and focused solely on the witches. It moved in that fluid, effortless manner that most supernaturals did as it floated down from the table to stand in front of the two women. It took one step forward, walking away from the shovel Jasmin had managed to drive into its body, letting the piece of hardware drop to the floor in a clatter.

The air around them was thick with spent magic, and the creature began to float closer toward the witches. Torie and Jasmin took a step back, each calling up power and channeling it to their hands. Abruptly, the apparition stopped, focusing on something behind the witches. It opened its mouth wide once again.

Both witches turned just as Michael stepped into the sunroom, his eyes wide and locked on the ghastly scene before him. The creature began to glow, light flickering throughout its frame as it launched itself at the man, reaching for him with limbs that seemed to stretch as they clawed the air.

Torie dove to one side out of the creature's path while simultaneously sending a wave of magic at Michael that knocked him backwards and to the side, sending him sprawling out of harm's way. The siphon slid by him, just missing his target, and floated into the kitchen. Torie and Jasmin followed it inside just in time to see it dissolve once again into a puddle of pulsating light, sinking into the floor and disappearing from view.

Jasmin rushed to Michael's side, offering her hand to help him off the floor.

"Are you okay?" she asked.

The man was definitely shaken, his hands trembling as he brushed himself off and regarded the witches.

"What...what just happened?" he asked.

"Um, well, you were supposed to stay in the car," said Jasmin, "and then nothing would have happened."

"That...what was that ghost doing here? I always heard it only haunts the grounds of The Sweetbriar," he stammered, squeezing the bridge of his nose between his forefinger and thumb to help clear his vision.

Torie frowned as she helped steady the man. "What are you talking about?"

"Surely you know The Sweetbriar is haunted," he said. "Everyone knows that."

"Well, we did hear a couple of people mention it," said Jasmin, "but we thought it was just part of the local charm."

"Charm? What's charming about a ghost?" Michael questioned. "People have seen it, floating around the pond and the grounds there."

Torie and Jasmin stared at one another.

"Are you saying that thing is what has been haunting The Sweetbriar?" asked Torie. "How long has this been going on?"

Michael shrugged, the motion extending into a shoulder roll to work the kinks out. "As long as I can remember. Everyone knows to stay away from that place...well, everyone except the tourists. Say, what did you hit me with? How did you do that?"

Torie took a deep breath, rubbing the man's shoulders but not answering his questions. The mystery was beginning to deepen. Why would a siphon attach itself to one of the east coast's most prominent bed and breakfast establishments?

Chapter Twenty

Torie sat in the back of Sheriff Odette's squad car waiting for the man to finish questioning Jasmin. The sheriff had separated them upon arrival at the scene, preferring to get each statement alone. Torie could understand his reasoning, but she didn't like the vibe she was getting from the police officer. He seemed a bit too eager to separate the women and hit them with rapid fire questions.

"Should we get our stories straight before Odette gets here?" Michael had asked.

"There's nothing to get straight," Torie had answered. "Just tell him what happened and nothing more. Maybe just don't go into great detail about certain aspects."

"That won't be hard considering I don't really know what I saw," he had replied.

Now, sitting in the back of a potentially corrupt police officer's car, Torie thought maybe they should have corroborated what they were going to say. Her mind played and replayed what had happened in that room a dozen times. No matter how hard she tried, there was too much information missing for her to piece together a strategy moving forward.

Why would the siphon kill James Keller? Was it just coincidence that it happened after Torie and Jasmin had found out the old reporter had been the only person cataloguing the string of disappearances and deaths? Was the siphon responsible for the death of Samantha Perry as well? If so, why hadn't her body been as desiccated-looking as James Keller's?

All the questions came back to the siphon. They simply didn't know enough about the creature to form a plan of action. Anytime they had faced the supernatural in the past, they had an idea of what they were up against. But this thing was something new; and until they learned more about what it was, they had a blind spot that could prove very dangerous.

A thought sprang into her head, a plan that was slowly forming. It was dangerous, and she knew Jasmin would probably not go for it, but it might be the only way to solve this situation. She was working the details out in her mind when the sudden, hard rap on the car window broke her train of thought, causing her to jump in surprise.

Sheriff Odette was standing outside her door and quickly pulled on the handle, then bent down, notebook in hand as he stared at Torie with dark eyes.

"So, I have statements from your two friends in there. You mind telling me what you were doing here?"

"Sheriff, do you know how many deaths have occurred in this county over the last fifteen years or so? Or how many odd disappearances there have been of people that just so happened to be passing through?" She hoped that by springing on the offense, she could diffuse whatever he was obviously plotting to throw at her.

It seemed to work as the big man was caught off guard by her questions.

"I don't see what that has to do with the fact that you and your friend seem to have a way of showing up around dead bodies in my town."

And there it was. He had tipped his hat, and Torie saw no reason in not beating him to the punch.

"Jasmin and I had nothing to do with this murder or any other in town. We were at the library much of the day with Michael when this was happening."

"Well now, I didn't say you were involved, but it's interesting that you went there. But why don't you tell me in your words what happened here?"

Torie told the sheriff how she and Jasmin had been researching any information they could find that could link Samantha's death to other strange deaths in the area. They stumbled across the reports about how many people passing through the area seemed to go missing, and that led them to the name of the reporter who seemed to be most familiar with the case. She pointed out that since they still had no car, Michael had been kind enough to drive them out to the farm where the reporter lived so they could speak with him. That's when they found the man's body.

The sheriff was nodding as she recounted her story, scribbling furiously with his pencil. He stopped, flipping back through his notes and rereading a couple of entries before turning back to Torie.

"So, you say you didn't see what happened to him?"

"You saw the condition of the body. It looked like he had been dead for a very long time."

Sheriff Odette nodded slowly. "Well, that's going to be up to the coroner to decide. But why were you looking into this in the first place?"

Torie narrowed her eyes. "To help Emily. I told you, I don't believe she did this, and we are getting together as much information as possible...for the lawyer."

"I see," said the sheriff.

His tone told Torie that he didn't see and didn't believe a word she just said.

"If you don't have any other questions for me, may we please leave? This has been a very trying day and I need to take a long, hot bath," Torie said.

The sheriff stood up, drawing himself to his full, impressive height. Standing above her, his Stetson cast a shadow over his eyes, making him impossible to read. "Oh, there will be more questions, I'm sure. But I need to wait for the coroner's preliminary report on what happened here. I'll be in touch."

Great, she thought, stepping out of the car and heading towards Jasmin and Michael, who were waiting on the porch.

"You guys alright?" she asked.

"We're fine," Jasmin answered. "For now." She gave Torie a look that let her know they were probably thinking along the same lines.

"Yep. I'm worried about what the coroner might find this time," added Torie. "Come on, let's get back to The Sweetbriar. Something tells me we need to regroup."

The drive back to the library happened in near total silence. There were things Torie needed to speak with Jasmin about but wasn't sure how much to say in front of Michael. As it turned out, she didn't have to worry about keeping their secret. As they pulled up to the library and climbed out of the truck, he turned to the two women.

"So, what exactly are you? Despite what I said to Sheriff Odette, and the fact that I don't know what I saw back there, I know that I saw The Sweetbriar ghost and the two of you fighting it with...superpowers."

Jasmin turned to the man. "They weren't superpowers."

"It was magic," said Torie. "Jasmin and I are witches, but we don't advertise that." She ignored the stern look from Jasmin. "As a matter of fact, there is something you might be able to help us with. Jasmin will be happy to tell you more, but can you help her do some research on the history of The Sweetbriar ghost?"

She turned to Jasmin, who was looking at her as if she had suddenly grown a second head.

"Look, we don't have a lot of time here," said Torie. "If the sheriff and the coroner can cook up evidence that Emily was involved in the killing of Samantha Perry to protect...whatever, then do you really think they won't do the same to us? You find out what you can about that siphon, I'm going back to The Sweetbriar to look around."

She was swinging a leg over her bike when Jasmin stopped her.

"Do not do anything stupid. And be careful...someone is controlling that thing, and we've now lost any element of surprise when it comes to stopping it."

Torie nodded and gave her friend's hand a squeeze. "You be careful too. I'll see you back at The Sweetbriar."

Torie sat in her room, deep in thought. Their encounter with the siphon had left her more shaken than she cared to admit. It had managed to shrug off Jasmin's mystical attack. That meant it had magical defenses of its own, and if there was another encounter with the beast, getting through those defenses might mean the difference between life and death.

Not that she was going to give up. That option had definitely crossed her mind though. Jasmin's car should be fixed in a day or so; that meant they could just wait it out and leave town. Head back to Singing Falls and no one would be the wiser. This was a human town, with human problems. Only, leaving someone...anyone...in danger, was not her style. Ever since she had discovered her magical abilities late in life, she knew there was a reason she had been chosen to receive those abilities. She wasn't going to let an innocent suffer, and she certainly wasn't going to let someone use a supernatural force to hurt other innocents.

Samantha Perry may not have been the most upstanding of citizens, but she didn't deserve what had happened to her. No one deserved that. And she certainly didn't deserve for her killer to be able to walk free. No. Torie was gifted her powers for a reason, and she intended to put a stop to whatever had been terrorizing this community for decades.

But to do that, she needed information that they probably didn't have access to in the town library. Information that she needed from her own library, hundreds of miles away. Jasmin's warning echoed in her mind.

Don't do it. You could end up who knows where.

She needed an anchor. Isn't that what Jasmin had called it? Jasmin could probably be her anchor, but that was assuming she would let her attempt what she had in mind. Plus, there might not be enough time. The sheriff could show up at The Sweetbriar at any moment with some kind of fabricated nonsense and try to arrest her.

No. If she was going to do this, she had to do it now.

A thought struck her, and she made her way to the desk in her suite, grabbing for her purse. She fumbled around at the bottom of her bag until her hand closed around something smooth and hard. She lifted her hand and opened her fist to reveal the black Hypersthene stone Emily had given her. Immediately, she felt her racing thoughts begin to settle, and her mind found clarity and strength of purpose. What was it Emily had said to her about this stone?

"They are for grounding oneself during deep meditation."

Torie made her way to the bedroom and sat down on the floor, drawing her knees in and crossing her ankles. Instantly, she felt a jab in her lower right buttock as her sciatica reminded her of all the biking she had done in the last couple of days.

"Nope, not happening," she said, standing to sit on the edge of the bed. "I can meditate sitting here as easily as I can on the floor."

She held the Hypersthene in her hand and lowered her head until her chin rested on her chest. Focusing on her breathing, she willed the world around her to slowly drop away. The sounds of the old house as it creaked and settled around her slowly faded away, taking with it the ambient voices of the staff and guests who murmured incessantly in the background. The smell of fresh fruit and jams fell away until there was nothing for her senses to perceive. There was only a void, and it permeated every inch of the space around her.

When all was quiet, and darkness wrapped itself around Torie like an old friend, she allowed a single thought to intrude on her perfect peace.

Home.

The thought flowed over her, wrapping her body in warmth and safety. But not just home. She concentrated on her library; the feeling of total and complete happiness when she stepped inside, surrounded by her mother's books and all the things that made her feel content. She imagined sitting in her favorite chair, the oversized, plush, red-plaid blanket suffusing her body in warmth. The fireplace crackling, threatening to smother her in the scent of burning wood that she loved so much. And all of it permeated by the scent of worn leather and old paper, just waiting to surrender secrets to her that had been long lost in time.

She focused on that space, letting her mind lock onto it, until she felt her physical body dissolve, falling away as it tumbled through space and time. She could feel the outside world rushing by but was afraid to open her eyes. Instinct told her if she fixated her vision on anything while she felt like her body was in motion, she would freak out and stop drifting. She had to stay calm, stay focused on the task at hand.

To her, it felt like she was in the grips of a vertigo she could control. She felt the sensation of movement, while being in control of everything around her. It wasn't until she stopped moving, when the earth settled around her, that she dared open her eyes.

And when she did, she was standing in her library, looking at the trove of books that covered the custom floor-to-ceiling bookcases she had so carefully constructed for her favorite room in the house.

Looking down, she had the strangest feeling of Deja vu. She couldn't really describe the feeling; of course, she had been in her own home before, but the feeling of being in two places at once was most akin to that of Deja vu. Being back in her house made her think of Elric, and Leo, and even Fionna. She almost doubled over as everything started to shift once more. Everything around her felt like it was starting to move again, and she could feel her body begin to slip.

Focus. Home. Library. That was all she needed to feel

steady, and once again the room came into focus. The book-cases held more books than she cared to count, and she had no idea how long she would be able to tether herself there. Certainly not long enough to go through each tome looking for specific information.

She closed her eyes and steadied herself, then held out one hand as she spoke a single word.

"Siphon."

The air hummed with the power of her calling, and instantly an old, worn, red leather book flew to her hand. She smiled, just as she heard a voice come from downstairs.

"Hello? Is someone up there?"

It was Elric. He was there, and his was the equivalent of a soothing balm after being in the hot sun for too long. She sensed his movement, the way he carried himself on the balls of his feet when he was on high alert. She could hear him bounding up the stairs in great leaps.

As much as she wanted to, she couldn't let him see her. She couldn't see him. If she did, she might not be able to get back to Jasmin.

Her body glowed with power as she steadied her mind, thinking about her suite at The Sweetbriar. Pushing the images of Elric out of her mind. She panicked, thinking it might already be too late, but then she remembered her stone.

Her grounding element.

She envisioned the stone, forced her mind to recall the texture of it in her hand as she willed herself to return to the inn. She dissolved away in a soft nimbus of falling light just as the door to her library swung open.

Chapter Twenty-One

A wave of nausea passed over her as she settled back into her surroundings at The Sweetbriar. Opening her eyes, she waited until the room settled completely before attempting to stand. For a moment, she felt like she sometimes would upon first waking and sitting up too fast in bed. But without all the aching joints and back pain.

The feeling passed and she looked down at the book in her hands. It was a book of handwritten spells, many of them in her mother's handwriting. The pages were yellowing, but the ink on them was still legible.

Opening the book, she set about trying to sift through the pages for the information she needed. She knew enough about how her calling magic worked to know that just because she had called out the word siphon, that might not be how the creature was referred to in this book of spells. Her magic was powered by her intent and subconscious needs. Therefore, what she now sought out could be listed in any number of ways.

Nearly an hour went by in the blink of an eye, and she

was so enraptured in reading that she barely noticed her door open. She looked up just as Jasmin carefully entered the bedroom.

"Oh, there you are," her friend said. "I was knocking outside, and you didn't answer. I thought maybe you were asleep. I found something at the library that I think you should see."

"Good, because I have something to show you as well. But you go first." She motioned for Jasmin to take a seat next to her.

"Okay, so I was trying to research any leads, find any information that could help us, and Michael was babbling on about something when he mentioned that it had been really hard on he and Cameron when the Perrys purchased control of the supply chain for the coffee shop. That was why he had taken on a second job at the library to help pay for things until they can get past this bottleneck the Perrys have them in.

"So that started me thinking. I wondered what else the Perrys have been buying around here. The shell company they used to buy the supply chain that feeds a lot of stores around here, had also made a few other purchases, but nothing major. Then, a search came back linking Samantha Perry to a land purchase. A big one. One that she used her own name and money for. She bought over a hundred acres in the western corner of the state. And the deed to the property had her name and that of Jacob Perry on it."

"They were more than just a little involved. This wasn't just an affair," Torie said. "If they were setting up house together, and Walter found out..."

"Then he would be facing more than just a company bankruptcy. The personal fallout from something like this could have ruined any future businesses. All those fat Wall-street execs he makes deals with would have shunned him. Not out of solidarity with his wife of course; more like fear of their own wives starting to dig too deeply into whatever they try to keep hidden."

Torie's mind was spinning at the news. This could definitely explain why Samantha had dropped her efforts at developing the town; she was going to be relocating to this area, and the thought of bulldozing her new hometown wasn't sitting right with her. She was about to burn her bridge to big society; it wouldn't do to try and re-establish herself on scorched earth here as well.

"Okay, your turn. What did you find?" asked Jasmin.

Torie patted the book on her lap. She had one finger crooked into the top of it, holding the page she was on when Jasmin had entered the room.

"I may have just found out some information about the siphon. Which hopefully includes a way to destroy it."

Jasmin eyed the book suspiciously. "Torie. Where did you get that book?"

Torie bit her lip, shifting her weight from side to side as she considered the best way to answer that.

"Well, it's from my mother's collection of mystic books that she left behind."

Jasmin frowned. "The ones in your library?" Her eyes widened, and her voice rose an octave. "At your house? How did it get here?"

"Umm, actually, I...went to retrieve it." Torie closed her eyes, expecting a verbal onslaught that didn't come. When she opened her eyes, she saw a look on Jasmin's face that she wasn't used to. It was a look of fear.

Jasmin took her by the hand, squeezing hard. "Torie, I told you how dangerous drifting is...even for someone seasoned at it. You could have...I could have...you could have been lost. And had that happened, there would have been no way for even me to have found you and brought you back."

Torie frowned, squeezing her friend's hand. "But I wasn't lost. I made it back just fine. And yes, I knew the risks; but I also know the risks these people take if we don't find a way to stop that thing. I was picked to have these powers for a reason, Jasmin. I will never put my well-being ahead of that of an innocent."

Jasmin stared at Torie then just shook her head. Finally, she reached over and grabbed her, pulling her head to her chest as she hugged her close. "You are a stubborn thing. One of these days, you're going to find yourself in a situation you aren't ready for if you keep doing this."

Torie let her squeeze her for a moment more then laughed. "Yes, but I'm pretty sure I'll have you there to pull my fat outta the fire."

Jasmin exhaled a deep breath and broke contact. "Okay. Show me what was so important that you had to risk your very existence to get it."

Torie breathed deep and opened the book. "I was only there for a split second, so I called to the books, asking for one that contained information about a siphon. This is the one that came to me out of all of them. Just now, I found an entry about soul globes, or soul gobblers; that's what my mother called them. It is a vessel created to contain the essence of living beings. The more souls trapped inside it, the more powerful it gets."

"That would explain why it was able to shrug off our magic," said Jasmin.

"Yes, and not only that, but it also says that the globe is subject to the whims of its creator. It is basically just a machine, created to harvest souls, thus allowing the real benefit of that power to be passed onto the person who built it. There is a way to destroy it with hex magic, but there are certain rare earth elements we need to gather, and I have no idea what some of them are."

"First things first, what kind of benefits does it pass on to its creator?" Jasmin asked.

Torie thumbed a few pages, running her finger down the one she settled on.

"It says here that collecting souls can transfer unlimited wealth, power to command lesser beings and make them your puppets, and the ability to..." she paused, the words on the page sinking into her mind.

"To what?" Jasmin pressed.

Torie slammed the book shut. "I know who the creator of the siphon is. Which means I probably know who the killer is as well." She was up, grabbing her purse to head out the door, Jasmin close behind her. "But first, we need to pay a visit to Emily Belmont at the jail, and hope the sheriff isn't there to stop us."

They skipped the bikes. Torie was able to convince Penny Henry that they needed to borrow her car. It was literally a matter of life and death they had told her. The car was an old Crown Victoria that sputtered and complained when the accelerator was mashed, but it got them to Trevor's auto shop/jail house infinitely quicker than they could have under pedal power.

Trevor was in the back and must have heard them pull up because he was walking towards the car, wiping his hands on a cloth, before they were fully out of the car.

"Torie, Jasmin, you shouldn't be here." His nerves were on full display as he kept looking over his shoulder towards the garage and the addition built onto the back of it. "If you're here to speak with Emily, I was given strict instructions that she is not to have contact with anyone."

"That is exactly why we are here, Trevor," Torie said. She marched right by the man, Jasmin on her heels, and headed for the back of the building.

Trevor hurried, shuffling his feet and wiping at the back of his neck with his rag.

"That's not a good idea. You don't want to get on his bad side. He can really make you miserable if he wants to," Trevor said. His tone was all over the place, but for the most part, he seemed to be pleading with the two women.

Torie looked back at him questioningly. "He's in there, isn't he?"

Trevor seemed to stammer, but before he could answer, Sheriff Odette stepped around the corner of the building, stopping the two women dead in their tracks.

"I thought I made it clear that no one is to see the prisoner without my prior approval." He crossed his arms over his chest, staring them down. "And I really don't remember giving you permission to be here."

Torie squinted at the man. She could feel her blood starting to boil and had reached her tipping point. She had known men like this before in her previous life; huge, bullying men who were forever trying to impose their power on women. She was done playing these games.

With a swipe of her arm, she exerted just enough power to sweep him against the side of the building and pin him there. She stepped forward, using her magic to lift him a foot off the ground as she looked up into his wild eyes. He tried to reach for his pistol, but she slammed his arm back against the wall.

Trevor made a move to intervene, but Jasmin placed a

hand gently on his arm, shaking her head and smiling at him.

"Okay, Sheriff, I was hoping it would not come to this, but it's time we have a little chat," Torie said. "My friend and I had absolutely nothing to do with either of the two murders that have recently happened in your town. But something tells me you know that. Just like you probably know that Emily Belmont didn't kill Samantha Perry. We believe the two murders are linked. Just like they are linked to an awful lot of other murders and disappearances that have happened around here for decades. The real killer is something you are not capable of dealing with. But we are. We have very special skillsets that make us uniquely qualified to deal with this."

She held up one hand and summoned a ball of fire to float above her palm. Holding it close to the sheriff, she saw him squirm as the flame sizzled and turned in the air.

"What we are hunting, is something you need to stay away from. Let us handle it, and I promise you, your town can go back to being the sleepy, bucolic slice of Americana that it is. And you can go back to collecting your fat checks from your family and padding your secret bank account." She saw his eyes widen even further and smiled. "Yes, we know all about that. We also know you would do some questionable things to keep that gravy train rolling. Not murder...we don't think you did that; but you would definitely try to keep this quiet and possibly blame it on someone innocent just to get it to go away.

"But here's the thing; it's not going to go away if you send Emily Belmont away for something she didn't do. So, here's what's going to happen next. Jasmin and I are going in there to speak to Emily, and then we are going to leave. You are going to speak to that coroner of yours and have him turn over the real files on the case, not the doctored one. Then, you're going to have him fired. As for you and your future... Well." She held the flame closer to his squirming form. "We trust you'll do the right thing." She released her magic and let him drop to the ground.

Jasmin joined her as they walked by the man.

"And what if I say no to all that?" he sneered at them.

Jasmin paused and turned around, a glint in her eye. "Then I know a spell that will wipe all of this from your mind, no harm, no foul. But...I can't be certain how deeply the spell will go. It could erase only your most recent memories of this, or it could hollow you out back to infancy. I haven't done it in so long, I can't remember how it will actually work." She smiled, her eyes flashing yellow magic as the sheriff backed away, suddenly finding it hard to swallow.

"Now, if you'll excuse us, we have a monster to slay."

Chapter Twenty-Two

The door gave way to Torie's wishes as the two women entered the holding room. Emily was sitting on her cot and leapt to her feet when she saw them walk into the room. She grasped the cell bars, standing as close to the women as possible.

"Torie! What are you doing here? You know you'll get in trouble for this," she said.

"Don't worry about that," Torie responded. "We're here because we need your help. Step back."

Emily did as she was asked, moving away from the cell door as Torie placed a hand on the latch system and popped the door open. She ignored Emily's wide-eyed stare as she and Jasmin stepped into the tiny space.

"How did you do that?" Emily asked, looking from the door latch to Torie. "I mean how *exactly*? I know you aren't...normal."

"With magic," Torie replied. "Real magic. Jasmin and I are witches, and we can do a lot more than just open locked doors." She moved over to sit on the small cot and motioned for Emily to have a seat next to her. "We've been looking into your case, trying to find something that will prove your innocence. Well, we certainly found quite a bit, including the fact that there is an element of the supernatural at work here."

Emily looked from one woman's face to the other. "You don't think I have anything to do with that, do you? I swear, despite what people around town might say, I don't have any magical abilities."

"We know that," said Jasmin. "You have an affinity for nature, and you may well register higher on the psychic aptitude scale than most, but you're not a witch."

"Then what do you need me for?" she asked.

Torie cleared her throat and turned to face the woman. "Emily, someone in this town has created a creature capable of stealing souls from the living. This creature is under the control of someone very dangerous, and we have to stop them. But we had an encounter with this creature, this siphon, and it's more powerful than we expected. There is a way to destroy it, but that's where you come into play." She stopped and withdrew a piece of folded paper from her pocket and showed it to Emily. "In order to destroy it, we need these items. Now we can get everything with the exception of powdered Adder tongue, pieces of newly hatched eggshells, and this one...pure extract of feverfew...we have no clue where to get this."

"Well, feverfew is found in most varieties of daisies," she said, "but if you need the pure form, that's a little different. Feverfew is native only to western Asia and the Balkans. Not easy to come by."

"Great," said Torie with a sigh. "Can I drift that far?"

Before Jasmin could nix that idea, Emily spoke up. "I said it was not easy to come by, but it's not impossible. I have some in my shop. But only a little. It's extremely rare, as you can imagine. I also have the Adder tongue as well. But you'll have to find the newly hatched eggshells elsewhere."

"I can help with that." It was Trevor's voice. He was standing outside the cell watching the three women. "I mean, unless it's some weird kind of animal you need it from."

Emily smiled kindly at him and shook her head. "From what I understand, newly hatched eggshells are used in spells to replicate the power of a newborn soul that has yet to be contaminated by anything earthly."

Jasmin looked at her admiringly. "Very good. And yes, it doesn't matter what comes out of the egg. We just need the shells."

Trevor nodded slowly. "There's a chicken farm on the other side of town that I deliver mail to. I can get you some shells from there. The lady who owns it raises baby chicks to sell at the town fair. She should have some newborns any time now."

"Good," said Torie. "The sooner you get them the better. As in tonight if possible. Jasmin and I will head to Emily's shop to get the rest of the items needed for the spell to take this thing out." She turned to face Emily. "Unless you'd like to come with us?" She looked from Emily to the open cell door.

Emily sighed deeply. "I really hate sitting here. But I'm not going to risk becoming a fugitive from the law at this point. Clear my name. Make them release me legitimately."

Torie nodded, admiring the woman's strength. Had the situation been reversed, she was pretty sure she wouldn't be able to tolerate sitting in that cell. All this did was once again renew her resolve to see Emily freed and her name cleared. They left the cell, and Torie closed the door behind her but did not reengage the locking mechanism.

As they were walking out, the sheriff was standing at the door to the jail and stepped aside as they approached.

Torie hesitated and then turned to face him. "This thing knows we are onto it. It also knows what we are. I think that's why it killed James Keller before we could talk to him about what he knew regarding its activities over the years. He obviously knew something and was trying to stay low; that's why he didn't post anything regarding Samantha Perry's death. He wasn't about to get any further involved. So, if I'm right about that, then it might come here to try and take out Emily. Guard her with your life. I'm depending on you."

She gave him a look that let him know she wasn't asking for his help. They made their way to the old Victorian and peeled out of the gravel lot, turning onto Main Street.

The sun had moved, casting long shadows over the storefronts as they pulled into a parking space just in front of Emily's crystal store. Squinting against the low sunlight, they could make out Cameron as he walked up the sidewalk, his eyes locked on them.

"Looks like someone had a talk with their husband," Jasmin said as they exited the vehicle.

Torie took a deep breath as Cameron approached them. She held up both hands.

"Why didn't you tell me?" he asked, hands on his hips. "You told Michael, but not me?"

"Michael wasn't supposed to know anything," Torie said. "But he didn't stay in the truck."

"Yeah, he said he was almost killed by The Sweetbriar ghost."

Jasmin rolled her eyes. "He was perfectly safe. The ghost was only focused on us."

"Not from the way he described it," said Trevor, before wrinkling his brow and then rolling his eyes. "Of course, Michael has been known to embellish a little for dramatic effect."

"Look, I promise we will talk about this, and we'll tell you all that we can," said Torie. "But right now, we need to get into Emily's store to get some things we are going to need later tonight." She glanced out at the setting sun. "And we don't have a lot of time. That's not a ghost inhabiting The Sweetbriar. It's something a lot more dangerous, and we need to stop it."

Trevor nodded, stepping aside. "What do you need me to do?"

"Nothing. Stay away from The Sweetbriar tonight," said Jasmin.

Torie held up a finger. "Actually, if you really want to help, get Michael and the two of you go over to the jail where Emily is being held. The sheriff is watching over her, but I'd feel comfortable if someone was watching over him as well. Plus, you and Michael should stick together until this is over."

Trevor frowned. "I thought you said that thing was only after the two of you."

"Can't be too careful," Torie said, turning away from him.

Jasmin was already at the door and had blown it open. The two of them walked in and headed for the area where Emily had said they would find everything they needed. Torie grabbed a large, cloth shopping bag and began filling it with the items. She watched as the sun slowly dropped along the horizon. They had a trap to set, and not a lot of time in which to do it.

Everything they were planning hinged on them getting the killer to show their hand and summon the creature. As ever, Torie was reminded that the real monsters out there were often made of flesh and blood and yet had lost all touch with their humanity.

Chapter Twenty-Three

Inside The Sweetbriar, it was unnaturally quiet. Or maybe not, considering most of the guests were still reeling from the news that one of their family members had been murdered. Torie had expected them to clear out once the tragedy had been discovered. Maybe head back home, make arrangements for the funeral, deal with their emotional tidal wave that was sure to sweep over them after such devastating news.

But no. That didn't happen. They were all staying put, waiting to hear when and if Emily would be fully charged for the murder. Waiting for the lawyers to call and let them know what their next move should be. And waiting for the sheriff to lift the order that no one was to leave town until the investigation was closed.

This was surprising in that he was basically in their back pockets, but Torie assumed that he needed to mostly follow the standard operating procedure when investigating a death— even if he had already decided who the murderer was. Hopefully, what he had witnessed at the jail had given him pause to reconsider what he was doing, but Torie wasn't putting much faith in that. The only thing at that moment she believed in was the woman striding into the inn next to her, and the bag of ingredients they had gathered that would allow them to destroy a creature that should never have been allowed to exist.

Jasmin must have sensed her thoughts because the concern she voiced was along the same lines.

"You know, we are going to have to deal with the person who created this monster as well," she said. "I don't even know how a human would have been able to do it. But whatever they did, the knowledge they have is too great to risk them being able to do it again."

Torie didn't say anything. She knew the seriousness of what had happened, but still, she wanted to know why someone would do this. There was no possible reason for taking human lives and using their souls for personal gain. There just wasn't. She would do whatever was needed to stop this madness.

Even if it meant hurting a friend.

The sound of heels clicking across the floor snapped her out of her thoughts just as Penny walked out of the check-in office, waving to the two women.

"Torie! Jasmin! There you two are. We missed you for the dinner hour. Do you want us to set something up for you on the terrace? We had duck roasted in a peach and orange reduction. It was so good," she said.

The two women smiled.

"No, we have already eaten, but thank you for thinking of us. Hey, can you do me a favor? I need you to stay in your room tonight, no matter what you hear. Can you do that?" Torie asked.

Penny gave her a perplexed look. "What do you mean? Why would I do that? Is this about what happened—"

"Because you look like you're exhausted from all the hard work you put in all day. Wouldn't you like to have a good night's rest?" said Jasmin. She lightly touched the older woman on the arm, sending the tiniest sliver of magic into her.

Penny frowned, blinking away her sudden confusion. "You know, I am rather tired and think I'll turn in early tonight."

Jasmin smiled and patted her lightly on the shoulder. "That's a good idea. And you know, I bet Henry would like to join you. Where is he? We'll find him and send him on up to you."

She nodded slowly, turning towards the stairs. "He's out back setting the nets around the new apple saplings we planted. Those pesky deer will eat them to nothing if they can get at them." She was on the stairs, moving slowly and waving goodnight to them over her shoulder.

"Nifty trick," said Torie. "You're going to have to show me that one after we get home."

"First, we take care of business here. Should we do this outside?"

"Let's use the workspace in the kitchen. I don't think we'll run into anyone in there. Plus, we need a pestle and mortar for this, so what better place to find one."

Together, they made their way into the expansive kitchen and placed the bag of mystical ingredients onto the large center island. Torie emptied it onto the work surface while Jasmin set about rifling through the cabinets to find the items they needed. By the time she made her way back to Torie's side, all the items they had collected were on display.

Torie used her magic to call to the book of spells she had retrieved, and it appeared in her hand in a flash of light. She found the page that was bookmarked and laid it open before them.

"I wonder if this is like making explosives or anything like that," Torie said. "You know, one wrong calculation or misstep and boom."

Jasmin shrugged. "Creating this type of magic was never my thing. I can follow a spell book as well as anyone, but when it comes to putting together concoctions...your guess is as good as mine."

The steps were pretty clear, and they began work by grinding the eggshells into a powder and adding the Adder tongue. Crystalized secretions from a green toad as well as dried petals from a dragon fruit plant were then dropped in as well. After mixing everything carefully, they came to the last ingredient, the super rare feverfew extract. This part called for the addition of an incantation as it was dropped into the mix.

"*Expedia tempur, morandis acai,*" Torie whispered as she dropped the feverfew into the mix.

Smoke billowed out of the mortar, but rather than stinging the eyes, it had a pleasant aroma that made the witches think of burning wood from a newly lit winter fireplace. The smoke climbed to the ceiling of the kitchen, swirled itself into a ball, and then retreated back into the bowl, turning the contents into a glowing powder that pulsed with power.

"So, this is how humans do magic," said Jasmin. "Can you imagine not being able to just speak our power into being and having to go through this to accomplish the most mundane of acts?"

"Thank goodness my mother knew more about this

stuff than I probably ever will. First thing I'm doing when I get home is organizing that library and studying her books," replied Torie. "Do you have the satchel?"

Jasmin reached into the small bag she carried and withdrew a small, gossamer-thin woven bag with a silver cinch drawstring. It was the last thing they had taken from Emily's shop, and together, they carefully added the contents of the mortar into it, then closed it tightly.

"Okay," said Torie. "Showtime."

Together, they left the kitchen and headed for the terrace. Moving across the stone space, they headed for the stairs that would lead them to the grounds. To the left of the landing was the vegetable garden for the property and to the right, the fruit orchards bloomed. Straight ahead would have taken them to the paths that led to the mineral ponds and hiking trails.

They headed for the fruit trees, and almost immediately could hear the sound of voices. They stepped into the grove of trees and could just make out Brad Henry in the distance. His tone was one of pleading, and they could hear the sobs in his voice.

"...I can't do that. I don't know what more you want from me. Please..."

The man was on his knees and seemed to be pleading with someone just out of their view.

Torie and Jasmin stepped into the space and called out in his direction.

"Mr. Henry...don't move, stay where you are," said Torie. "There was a shuffling sound, and they could see someone else start to dart off, heading for the darkness of the tree stands. "Kitty! Don't run from us. We really aren't in the mood to chase you."

The figure stopped and slowly turned around. She was

wearing a large raincoat that obscured her form with a hood that hid her face. But when she pulled back the hood, Kitty's face came into view as the witches approached them.

"Well, looks like the Kitty's out of the bag," said the woman, a cruel sneer spreading across her features. She glared at Henry. "Did you tell them?"

The old man shook his head fervently. "I swear, I haven't told a soul. Not even Penny knows."

Torie looked from one to the other. "Why don't we just talk this through? I'm sure we can find some peaceful way to resolve things."

Kitty laughed. "Peaceful resolve? With two witches? I'm assuming that's what you are, right?"

Neither Torie nor Jasmin answered as they inched forward.

"No matter. You're not human, I know that much. That night at the pond, I saw your interaction with my reaper. I saw the magic you used." She pointed at Jasmin. "And then, at the old reporter's house, you two really showed your true colors."

"You were there?" asked Torie.

"I was out back watching the show. I can't be too far from the reaper to make it do my bidding. So yeah, I saw it all." She was fidgeting with something in her pocket but kept her hands hidden from view. "If you're wondering, the reporter wasn't my quarry. I just needed to make sure he didn't tell you anything he might have learned over the years about The Sweetbriar ghost. Of course, had the two of you had the decency to die that night in your rooms, it would have saved us all a lot of trouble."

"*You* tried to kill us that night?" said Jasmin.

Kitty smiled her awful grin again. "Well, technically it was Brad. But I made him do it."

"Had you been threatening Mr. Keller as well? Is that why he stopped reporting on all the disappearances and mysterious deaths in the area?" Jasmin asked.

Kitty nodded. "Yeah, he was digging a little too deep. So me and the reaper paid him a visit a few years ago and reached an...agreement. But I had a feeling you'd have gotten the truth out of him, so that was a loose end I had to tie up. But tell me, how did you know it was me?"

Torie took another small step forward. "I did some research into the reaper, as you call it. I learned that they are created by humans to do their bidding. They feed on the life essence of others and the human who controls them benefits from that in varying ways." She walked closer to Brad and Kitty. "One of those ways is health and extended life."

Kitty narrowed her eyes at the witch. "The picture in the registration office."

Torie nodded. "That isn't your mother in the picture with Brad's parents, is it? It's you. But why are you doing this? Why did you kill Samantha?"

"You answered your own question. These acts have let me live a long time...a healthy, long, life. But I could feel my energies waning; I needed a renewal. And the only way to do that was to feed my reaper another soul. With Samantha it was a crime of opportunity. She was out alone at the pond, and I took advantage. Simple as that. And now, I am on the verge of having the one thing I've always wanted. This house. This land will make me rich, and Brad here is planning to leave it all to me, right?" She cast a sideways glance at the old man still on his knees. "He and Penny were planning to retire, with a little push from me, and they are signing this place over to me."

"Is that what you want?" asked Torie, looking at Brad.

"We do want to retire, while we still have our health..."

"But you weren't planning on leaving it to Kitty, were you?" said Jasmin.

He didn't reply; his silence telling them his answer.

"But that was before the Perrys and all their money showed up. They were going to destroy this place and take the town with them," Kitty said. "I couldn't let that happen. I just couldn't. I've waited far too long for this. As owner of this property, just think of the new business I could attract."

A lightbulb clicked in Torie's mind just then. "That's it, isn't it? You're not interested in saving this town or the inn. You want more bodies coming here...more souls to feed to your reaper. Let me guess; it's requiring bigger and bigger sacrifices to keep up its end of the bargain with you, right?" Kitty didn't answer, she just glared at the witch. "That's the problem with things like this. There is always a price to pay, and that price does not remain fixed."

"Maybe not," Kitty said with a smile, "but I know one thing I bet you don't."

"And what's that?" asked Jasmin, moving to stand next to Torie.

"That your souls will provide more than enough power to keep my reaper going, and me young, for centuries to come."

With that, she moved quickly, taking a small silver whistle out of her pocket. Before either of the women could say anything, she raised it to her lips and blew. It produced no noise, but both Torie and Jasmin could feel the magic it gave off. In response, the trees behind them began to glow as the siphon emerged from the darkness.

Chapter Twenty-Four

There was no time to prepare a counter spell as the creature was on them before either could react. It had once again assumed a vaguely human form, long arms ending in transparent claws raked at the ground as it charged them. Once within reach, it lit up, captured souls flaring to life inside its monstrous form.

Raising one arm, it brought daggers down at the women, clearly intent on cutting them down. Before either of them could raise a shield, Brad Henry was in front of them, pushing both away just as the siphon's claw struck him, sending him flying like a rag doll.

Torie rolled to one side, her magic flaring to life as she sent a ball of fire searing at the siphon's head. The flames struck it, but aside from driving it back a few steps, did no damage. Torie was expecting this, and she switched tactics. She placed both hands on the ground in front of her, and let her power flow into the earth, searching until she found what she was seeking.

She called to the old growth that lived beneath the rich

soil surrounding the grove. Vines, older than the generations that worked the land itself answered her call and rose up, twisting their way around the siphon. They wrapped themselves around it, pulling it, holding it fast. Torie began to chant, using her magic to reinforce them, giving them the power to hold on even as the siphon attempted to dissolve and phase free of the vines. Sweat clung to her forehead as she struggled against the pull of the creature.

"Hurry, Jasmin! I don't know how much longer I can hold it."

Jasmin had reached into her pocket and held the cinched bag in her hands. She whispered to it, waking the power it contained.

"No!" screamed Kitty, seeming to sense what the witch was doing. She bent down and scooped up a rock on the run as she sprinted towards Jasmin's back.

Torie saw her aiming for her friend's head and she diverted just enough power to send a vine snaking across the ground to ensnare Kitty before she could strike Jasmin.

But while the diversion was enough to save her friend, it came with consequences of its own. Without her full might applied to the restraints, the siphon began to break free, inexorably snapping the vines that locked it in place. Just when Torie was certain she could not hold it, Jasmin threw the bag at the creature, watching as it swatted at the parcel, causing it to burst open.

This, however, the witches were prepared for.

Torie released the creature and raised both hands in conjunction with Jasmin. Together, their words sang out across the space.

> *"Unclean creature which stands before,*
> *we give you no place in magic or lore.*

May the all-seeing grace empower this spell,
and cloak this monster in a fragile shell."

The powder from the exploded bag danced around the beast as it swung its massive claws. Swirling about, the powder bonded to the witches' words and began to cling to the siphon, slowly encapsulating it in a second skin; one that hardened, locking the beast in place.

Kitty screamed, her rage ringing out across the field as she struggled in vein to free herself. Tears nearly blinded her as she watched Torie walk over to where she stood. The witch bent over and picked up the rock Kitty had attempted to strike Jasmin with.

Torie held it in front of her, then released it, dropping her hands to her sides. The rock floated in the air before her and she looked at Jasmin, nodding.

"Let those who are bound heed our plea,
and leave this realm as you please."

The rock wobbled in place, and then flew forward, striking the siphon in the center of its chest, shattering it into pieces. Fireworks burst forward as tiny bubbles of light escaped their prison. Torie watched as they turned and flitted through the air before rocketing skyward to disappear. All but two of the lights disappeared. A white light and a green light remained, and they floated over and hovered next to the fallen Brad Henry.

Jasmin knelt beside him and cradled the man's head in her arms. His body had been rent open by the siphon, and she hummed a bit of magic into his system that numbed him to the debilitating pain he was suffering. Torie made her way to them and knelt as well, looking up at her friend.

"Is there anything we can do?" she asked.

Jasmin shook her head as she failed to blink away tears and they ran freely down her face. She held his head and stroked his face.

Torie looked up at the lights, watching as they floated closer to Brad.

"That's it, isn't it," she whispered. "This is why you were helping Kitty."

Brad reached up clumsily, pawing at the light over his face. Despite the fact he knew he was dying, he smiled, his mouth falling open as he struggled to speak through gasped breaths.

"Mamma, Daddy...you're...free..." was all he was able to get out when a spasm of coughs tore into him. His breathing slowed and his rasping stopped until finally his body grew still in Jasmin's arms.

"No more pain, no more fight,
be joined as one, as you walk into the light."

Jasmin's voice was soft and buttery smooth as she chanted to the man in her arms. Slowly, a spark of blue rose from him, encircling the two others before they all shot upward, leaving the world of the living behind.

Jasmin turned to Kitty, her eyes blazing as she called power into her hands.

"Jas—no. This isn't the way. She has no power, she's no threat. She falls under human laws now," said Torie, placing a hand on Jasmin's arm.

Jasmin pulled free and held her hand out in Kitty's direction. The woman turned her head quickly, squeezing her eyes shut. She expected to be hit with a blast of magic, but instead felt her coat fly open and the silver whistle flew from her pocket into Jasmin's hand. The witch held it aloft, and Kitty watched as the whistle was vaporized in a swirl of white magic.

"There," Jasmin said. "Now she's harmless." She turned to Torie, who had her phone out, but then swerved back around to face Kitty. "Oh, and just so you know, without the siphon to grant you energy, everything it gave you will start to fade. So don't be surprised at how quickly your hair is graying."

A look of shock passed through Kitty as she held up a hand, her eyes widening at the rapidly encroaching wrinkles.

Jasmin looked at Torie. "We still need to call Odette. We need to deal with the body of Brad Henry. And maybe another, depending on how long it takes them to get here." She glanced at Kitty, who was already slumping over on the ground. "Looks like it won't be human law she answers to after all."

Chapter Twenty-Five

"How is she?" Torie asked.

Jasmin let out a deep breath. "She is inconsolable. Can you blame her? She just lost her husband of fifty years to a killer who has been living under the same roof as her for her entire adult life."

They were standing on the large front porch amid the flashing lights from Sheriff Odette's patrol car, an ambulance, and the town's firetruck. Torie had made sure Penny didn't see Brad's body. Jasmin had stayed with her in her bedroom after waking her from the sleep spell she had cast.

"Emily is with her now. She's hoping to stay with her until Penny's sister can get here from Florida," Jasmin said.

Once Torie had made the call to Sheriff Odette, he had made his way over to the inn along with the fire department and emergency services. Since the lock on the cell door hadn't worked since Torie had sprung it, Trevor had taken it upon himself to bring Emily over.

"She has a way with people," he had told them. "Penny

will need someone like that with her. Her whole world has just been turned upside down."

He had then left to go around to the back of the house, making his way to the orchard to help collect the body of Brad Henry. The EMTs were coming through the house, having managed to get a couple of stretchers back to the fruit grove. One of them had Kitty's tiny, fragile frame laid on it. Her drawn, wrinkled face was covered by a portable oxygen mask, and the blanket they used to cover her swarmed her small body.

Gray, rheumy eyes could barely focus on Torie and Jasmin as she was wheeled to the ambulance. Over the last hour, she had aged to the point she had lost her ability to speak.

Sheriff Odette walked up, notebook in hand, as they were lifting her into the ambulance.

"Do I even want to know what happened to her?" he asked.

"Let's just say she got what she's had coming. For a very long time," said Jasmin, giving the sheriff a sharp look. "Speaking of…how are you doing?"

He snapped his notebook closed. "I've spent the day thinking about things. I've decided that it's in my best interest to…retire from my position as town sheriff. I've already tendered my resignation and will be leaving as soon as my replacement is up and running."

"And your replacement?" asked Torie, "is that going to be someone we need to be concerned about?"

The sheriff huffed, nodding his head in the direction of the EMTs wheeling out Brad's body. Trevor was assisting them, making sure they were careful moving his remains over the rough territory.

"Trevor will make a fine replacement. We talked, and he

agrees it's time he settled down to just one job. One that he really loves and can give his all to. I'll have him up to speed in a month."

"I have to say, I wasn't expecting that," said Jasmin. "But can he please get my car going before he takes on another role?"

Trevor was walking up just as she asked that question and laughed. "Couldn't help but overhear. Your car is available for pickup immediately."

Jasmin was visibly jolted at the news. "What? You got the part installed already?"

Trevor scratched his head. "Well, that's the thing. The part came in alright, but while I was waiting at the jail, I got bored, so I went to prep the car for install...and wouldn't you know it, it just...started right up. Everything that was broken, was...fixed. That was about the time Torie called to say the sheriff needed to come over here and to bring emergency services."

Jasmin frowned, looking at the perplexed young man. "How can that be?"

He shrugged, lifting his shoulder and holding them. "No idea. It's almost like it was just playing dead and decided enough was enough. Never seen anything like it." He walked away, shaking his head and muttering to himself.

"Well, looks like we can go home now," Torie said, moving to sit on the first step leading up to the porch. "But you don't look so happy about it."

"Oh no, I was just thinking about the car. Cars don't just heal themselves."

Torie shrugged, leaning back to rest on her hands. "Who knows. Maybe it really was just a loose connection, and all that fiddling Trevor did under the hood was just enough to get it going again."

"Maybe..." Jasmin replied, her words trailing off as she was lost in thought.

"Let's get to bed. I'm exhausted and we have a long day ahead of us tomorrow."

They made their way into the inn and up the stairs. Torie caught a glimpse of Millie Perry watching out her door, before her head quickly vanished back inside her suite, slamming the door after her. Briefly, she thought of checking in on the woman, but then decided she just didn't have the emotional energy to spare. Her bed was calling to her, and she could not wait to surrender.

The next morning, the sun streaming in through the curtains struck Torie, rousing her from a dreamless sleep. She cursed herself for having fallen asleep without closing the blackout blinds. But then again, had she done that, she might have slept on till midday. She showered, dressed, and made her way down to the dining room for some coffee. Of course, there was none, Penny was definitely not in shape to be up making breakfast for the inn and there was no Kitty anymore to help her.

Torie's mind turned briefly to the treacherous housekeeper. She wondered if the woman had survived the night. Judging from the speed with which she was deteriorating, Torie doubted she had even made it to the hospital. How had Sheriff Odette spun her case to the doctors there? If she passed on the way, had they even made it to the hospital? She had a feeling the sheriff had his own ways of dealing with things that might raise a lot of questions. She just hoped that wasn't something he would pass along to Trevor.

She decided to make her own coffee and made her way into the kitchen. To her surprise, she saw Jacob sitting at the table, absently stirring a small cup. She hesitated before clearing her throat to announce her presence as she entered the space, making her way to the cupboard.

"I'm sorry; I didn't mean to disturb you," she said. "I just wanted a cup for some coffee, but I can leave if—"

The younger Perry waved his hand and offered a weak smile. "No, of course not. If you're anything like me, you can't start the day without that caffeine fix." He looked away, his cheeks going red. "What am I saying? You're nothing like me. And I mean that in a good way."

Torie pulled out a chair and sat opposite the man. "How are you doing? How's the family handling everything?"

"Well, I'm sure you heard they caught the real killer last night. Walter has already left for the airport. He's going back to Chicago to try and salvage what he can of the business."

"And Millie?" Torie asked.

"She is on her way to the airport as well. She's filing for divorce and plans to take me for everything. But joke's on her...I'm not going to fight."

Torie let that hang in the air before nodding. "So, what about you, Jacob?"

"Me? I plan to stay here. Well, not here exactly, but I have a piece of land I purchased with Samantha. We were going to move here eventually to raise thoroughbreds. She had a thing for horses and decided it was time to leave the rat race of Chicago and this awful business we were trapped in. A business that fed off the hurt and misery of others, while making us fatter." Torie watched as he choked up a bit at the thoughts racing through his mind. He ran a hand over his face and sat back in the chair to compose himself. "They can't touch it...the land we bought. It was set up so that it is shielded from any legal garb by the company. I think I can learn to be happy here. Maybe."

He didn't say anything else, just sipped at the contents of his cup, occasionally blowing lightly across the top of it. Torie left him to his ruminations, deciding that she didn't want coffee after all.

Not much later, she was back downstairs again, this time with luggage and Jasmin in tow. They stood at the checkout desk with Emily on the other side of the counter. She wasn't sure how to check them out, so Torie swiped her American Express card and left them enough money to cover their stay plus a generous tip.

"And what are you going to do?" she asked, smiling at the woman while signing the guest book.

"Well, I was talking to Penny, and you know...I think I'm going to stay here with her until everything gets settled. Her sister is going to come up to help as well, so between us, we can maybe make a go at keeping this place running."

Jasmin arched her eyebrows at the news. "That's a surprise. What about your shop?"

Emily's eyes lit up almost as much as her smile. "Penny says I can have the space on the other side of the inn, that used to be Brad's workshop, to set up my crystal shop and sell from here. She thinks it might be a good way to draw in more business, and I think it's a win-win situation because I can then save up more money to one day open that pet shelter I've been dreaming about."

"Good for you," said Jasmin. "I think you're going to do great at whatever you put your mind to."

They said their goodbyes just as Trevor walked into the room, Jasmin's car keys swinging from one finger.

"Here you go, ladies. Your chariot awaits," he said, offering a mock curtsey in their direction.

Torie shook his hand, wrapping his in both of hers. "Thank you, Trevor, for everything. And congratulations on your new job. You're going to be great." She pulled him in, giving him a hug before heading out of the room.

Jasmin gave him a hug as well. "Take care, Trevor. And tell Cameron we said bye and thank you. We will definitely be seeing all of you again."

"Oh, you mean you're going to give this sleepy little town a second shot?" he said with a wink.

"Sleepy. Yeah, right," said Jasmin, swatting at the man before heading out to join Torie at the car.

They climbed inside and Jasmin fired up the engine, bringing the beast of a car to life.

"Sounds good as new to me," said Torie.

Jasmin nodded. "Yeah. It does, doesn't it? I still don't understand why it would just stop and then start running again on its own."

"Who knows. Maybe it was because we were meant to be here. You know what I don't understand? Kitty could have used that siphon for anything. She could have had it give her more money than she ever could have made from running the inn. Why go through all that?"

Jasmin gripped the steering wheel tighter before speaking. "I don't have the answers to that. But I think that people covet what they see every day to the point that eventually they develop a kind of tunnel vision. Maybe Kitty only ever saw The Sweetbriar as something she could never attain. She watched her parents work that place until it broke them. And all the while, there was a voice in the back of her mind whispering...one day. And then, that day came, in the form of a siphon."

"And that's the other thing. We still don't know how she actually built the siphon. We know how she controlled it, but where did it come from? Did she make it, or was it gifted to her? And if so...by who? Or what?"

Jasmin gave a long exhale. "We will probably never know the answer to that. And you're right. We did a very good thing. But you know what? Next time I suggest a five-star retreat in the middle of nowhere; slap me."

Torie laughed as they headed away from The Sweet-briar. "No kidding. As much as I'll miss some of the new friends we made, I am so looking forward to getting back home and sleeping in my own bed."

Jasmin gave her a quick glance and a sly smile. "You aren't fooling me. You're just looking forward to your naked weekend with Elric."

Torie blushed but only pursed her lips in response. If she had learned anything over the last few days, it was not to take the one you love for granted and enjoy every moment you had with them.

Even if that meant walking around naked for a weekend.

She glanced over at Jasmin and smiled. "Thank you, Jasmin. For always having my back, and always being there for me."

She turned and looked out the window at the country-side as it sped by. This had been the first girls' trip she had ever been on, and heavens willing, it would not be the last.

Chapter Twenty-Six

The crackling of the fire should have filled the space with warmth, but the blue and orange flames did the opposite, leaching heat from the stone walls and creating an eerie draft the sisters could feel in the depths of their bones.

The giant earthenware pot that sat over the flames was filled with a dark, viscous liquid that created an inky pool in which they gazed, watching an image play out. The image was that of two women, riding along a dusty road in a Jaguar convertible, laughing easily at their own jokes and enjoying their time together.

"You see, sister, she is strong," said one of the old women, her voice creaking and high pitched.

"Yes, you were right to test her. She was able to defeat the soul gobbler with little effort, and she definitely has the gift of sight. She may indeed be an excellent replacement for our fallen sister," replied the second woman.

Eyes as dark as the ichor in which they gazed scanned the room, landing on the figure of yet a third older woman, lying in a heap against the sandy walls. How long she had been lying there, they could not remember. That was how long they had been watching the fluid in their cauldron for signs of hope.

"She may not want to join us," said the first. "She seems to be incredibly attached to her life...and that of her friend, the other witch."

The second old woman nodded. "We can fix that if we have to. But she is the one. Young Torie will make an excellent Fate, my sister."

She waved a hand over the pot, dispelling the image and quieting the mystic flames that burned beneath it. Darkness reached out and pulled the two sisters into its grasp as they disappeared into the shadows.

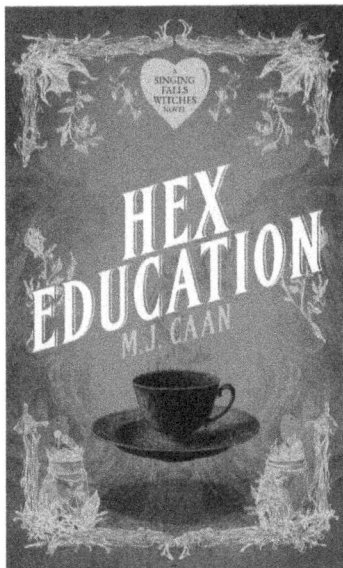

vinci-books.com/hexeducation

A witch's fresh start takes a dark turn when a body is found in Singing Falls.

Can Torie stop the evil threatening her town—and make an unimaginable choice? Magic, mystery, and danger await!

Turn the page for a free preview…

Hex Education: Chapter One

A single bead of sweat had formed on Torie Bliss' forehead. She peered deeply into the glass, holding her breath, scarcely daring to move in the slightest lest she disturb the powers-that-be whom had gifted her this one perfect creation.

At her side, Jasmin, her best friend and fellow witch, stood ready to assist at a moment's notice. They glanced carefully at one another, each feeding off the other's trepidation.

"So delicate," said Jasmin. "It's barely holding together. I'm not sure this is something we should even be attempting."

Torie shook her head. "No, this is the kind of offering that will put us on the map. I mean we're both good at this, but we need to take our skills to the next level if we're going to really succeed."

"I think we're setting ourselves up for attack with this one. I'm going to leave it to you. I'll find something else to offer up."

Torie didn't respond as she tentatively reached forward, willing her hand not to shake so as not to disrupt the delicate nature of what they had just created.

"Are you sure it's ready?" asked Jasmin, stepping slowly back from her friend.

Torie exhaled sharply, blowing a strand of hair free of her face. "We'll find out."

Carefully, she lifted the pan from the large gas burner of the stove. The large pancake soufflé they had created wiggled menacingly as she slowly moved it to the center island. It was a perfect cream color with an amber top.

"We can't sell this at the bakery," Jasmin said. "It's incredibly hard to make and time consuming."

"It's only hard for us to make because we aren't professional chefs. I'm certain that whoever we hire for the bakery will be able to whip these up in no time. And just think about the press we will get by offering them. No one has anything like this on their menu."

Jasmin looked around the kitchen. "It looks like a food cyclone moved through here. All just to create one pancake."

"It's not *just* a pancake. It's a statement piece. Anyone can make a pancake or a soufflé, but we will be combining the two into a masterpiece that everyone will want to try."

"Who is everyone?" Jasmin asked. "Cos this is Singing Falls. Everyone is going to want their pancakes with a bunch of butter and enough syrup running down them to drown a small child in. Ain't nobody got time for one giant pancake that takes forever to cook and serve." She then eyed the concoction suspiciously. "Now how are you going to get it out of the pan and onto a plate without destroying it? And you can't use magic because the cook most definitely will not be able to."

"Well, it should be set enough now that I can gingerly lift it to its final resting place, and then garnish it with some fresh whipped cream and an edamame thin wafer."

She ignored the look of horror on Jasmin's face as she set about carefully sliding a spatula under the tall cake and lifting it, and the mold it was cooked on, to the plate. Once it was resting, she carefully removed the metal ring from around it.

They both stepped back to admire the creation.

"There," said Torie. "Food as art."

"Well, it does look good," Jasmin replied, moving a little closer.

"It's perfect. Grab a fork and we are going to——"

She was interrupted by the front door opening and closing. Then, a giant box filled with canned goods entered the kitchen, followed by a tiny woman carrying said large box with surprising ease.

"Fionna! Watch out for the——" Jasmin started.

But she was too late. The box was well above Fionna's head, covering her field of vision. She dropped it onto the island, close enough to the pancake that the vibrations caused the soufflé to self-implode.

Torie stared in disbelief at the mound of perfectly whipped eggs and sugar, her fork held high in one hand. Jasmin struggled to contain her giggles, pretending to mourn the cake when Torie looked her way.

"Oh, hey guys," said Fionna, stepping away from the giant box of goods she had slammed down. "I didn't see you there. What's going on?"

She moved to stand next to them, following their eyes to the plate.

"Oh, what's that? Trying out new recipes?" She took the fork from Torie's hand and scooped up some of the flattened pancake and shoveled it into her mouth. "Um...this is good. Reminds me a bit of a pancake. Needs some syrup though."

Jasmin laughed as Torie's eyes flashed a vibrant blue before the magic settled back down within her.

"Did I say something wrong?" Fionna asked, her brown eyes widening above another mouthful of the pancake.

Torie let out a deep sigh. "Nope. Not a thing. So, you really like it?"

The squirrel shifter took another gulp and nodded. "It's a weird consistency, but pretty good." She looked around the kitchen. "What in the world happened in here? I know it didn't take all these dishes and mess to make that one little cake."

Jasmin stepped in, placing a hand on Torie's shoulder to steady her.

"You know, this might be a good time to test out some of the...renovations, we've been making to the house."

"It's a brand-new house," said Fionna. "What could you possibly have done?"

Jasmin offered a mischievous smile and gave her a wink. "It will be easier just to show you."

Torie nodded, and then turned to face the mess of dishes and mixing bowls in the sink, as well as the flour spills and drops of dried batter that decorated the range and countertops. She reached out one hand, twirling her forefinger in the air as she plucked at the magical threads that floated around the room.

Almost at once, the sink began to fill with water as the dishes began to clean themselves before floating into the waiting dishwasher. The pantry door swung open and a broom that was hanging from the wall danced out and began sweeping the crumbs onto a dustpan before floating to the trash can. Sponges began mopping at the spills on the countertop and the stove, while unused measuring utensils and baking cups rose and returned to their place in the cupboards.

Fionna watched, eyes fixed on the dancing dishes and cleaning tools all around her.

"So, you put a magic whammy on everything and turned it into that movie about that poor indentured girl with the evil stepmother and trashy sisters, huh?"

"What? No. There is no magical whammy. It was a very delicate and multi-layered spell that we cast to make this happen," said Torie.

"Well, it's kind of creepy. Did you enchant the mice and birds to do your laundry?" Fionna asked.

Torie crossed her arms. "Well, that would just be plain silly. Of course not. Besides, Leo ate the only mouse I've seen since moving in."

At the mention of his name, the little dragon zipped into the room, circling around to plop down on Torie's shoulder, his iridescent scales cascading from green to blue to yellow as he huffed into her hair, nuzzling his head against hers.

"Oof. You're getting too big for that," Torie said, reaching up to tickle his sides with her fingers.

"Hello, little Leo," Fionna said, wiggling her fingers at the dragon. His eyes lit up seeing her, and he immediately hopped from Torie's shoulder to run across the island, hopping into Fionna's arms. He folded his wings as she rocked him like a baby. "You just get cuter and cuter every time I see you."

"Huh. He's never that excited to see me," Jasmin said under her breath.

"It's a shifter thing," Fionna responded with a smile.

"Torie's not a shifter," Jasmin huffed.

"No, but she's his mommy. That trumps everything."

"Whatever," Jasmin replied, moving to inspect the giant box that Fionna had brought into the house. "Girl, what is in this?"

"Oh, there was a sale at the restaurant supply store, so I picked up a few things that we are going to need. And since the builders won't be out of the bakery for another week, I thought I'd leave them here until we can start moving stuff in."

"It…takes up a lot of room," said Torie. She reached over to push the box to the side and could barely move it. "Jeez, this thing weighs a ton. How are you just carrying it around like that?"

"Shifter strength," Fionna replied, her smile broadening. "I figure you have so much room here, surely you can find a place where it will be out of the way. And Elric can move it anywhere you need." Her eyes sparkled at the mention of Elric's name. "Speaking of…how are things going with the big, bad wolf?"

Torie cast her a glance out of the corner of her eye as she turned to check on the progress of the magical cleanup. "Things are going great. I couldn't be happier."

"Has he officially moved in?" Fionna asked.

Torie shook her head. "Not yet. But we are getting there."

"Uh oh," said Jasmin, moving to stand next to her friend. "I know that tone. What's wrong?"

Fionna sat Leo down and casually lifted the giant supply box from the island to the floor, so she had an unobstructed view of her friends. "Is something wrong? Between you and Elric?" she asked.

Torie tried to will away the redness she felt creeping up

her neck. There was no point in lying; Jasmin knew her too well, and Fionna had the senses of a lie detector.

Torie offered a wan smile. "Honestly, everything is really good. I have never met a man more attentive, loving, devoted or dedicated to me in my life. He's pretty much perfect."

Jasmin frowned. "No one is perfect, Torie."

"Well, he's pretty darn close, then." She turned back, just as the last dishes marched into the washer and it started itself. She moved to inspect the stove as the sponges finished their cleanup work and headed into the sink to scrub themselves clean. "But I'm not always sure such blind devotion is good for us. I mean, he's like a big old knight in hairy armor; and I don't always need saving."

Both Jasmin and Fionna stared at her, crossing their arms, lips pursed.

"What? You look like you want to say something," Torie said.

"It's just weird hearing you say something like that when you're just as guilty of it as he is," said Fionna.

Torie stared hard at her friend, eyes narrowed. "What are you talking about?"

Jasmin turned and pretended to busy herself with directing the sponges back to their drying racks, and then opening the range door to inspect the inside of Torie's oven. Fionna, eyes narrowed, gave her a steely look before returning her attention to Torie.

"Well…it's just that, you know, you kind of have to be the big protector of everyone you meet. And there is absolutely nothing wrong with that, but you seem to think that you must protect and save everyone. Even if it means striking out on your own to do it."

Torie started to speak but then pursed her lips and

regarded her friend. Leo was sitting up on his hind legs on the island, paying rapt attention to Torie. His emerald-green eyes flicking back and forth between her and the squirrel shifter.

"Sure, I feel a certain responsibility to my friends. Why is that so bad?"

"No one is saying it is," replied Fionna. "It's just that we need you to know that, as strong as you're getting, you don't have to shoulder all the responsibilities for everyone around you. The day is going to come when you're going to have to give in and trust someone else to do the heavy lifting for you."

Torie started to answer but Jasmin interrupted. "Torie, you might just be the strongest hex witch I've ever met, but you can't be everywhere at once. And when that day comes, just know that we'll have your back. And remember, Elric's a good guy. Maybe you guys can learn to cut each other some slack in the who needs to save who category and just…enjoy that you've found one another."

"Speaking of," said Fionna, tilting her head to one side.

A few seconds later, the front door opened and closed again, and Elric walked in, a large bouquet of flowers in one hand. He smiled at everyone and presented them to Torie with a quick peck to her forehead.

"Aww," said Jasmin, giving Torie a knowing glance. "What a good guy."

Elric frowned, but any questions he may have had were smothered as Torie wrapped her arms around him in thanks.

"My big, strong man," she said. "Speaking of, can you please take this to the pantry for me?" She indicated the large box Fionna had brought in.

"Oh, and here I thought you were happy to see all of

me, not just my muscles," he said playfully, picking up the box and heading for the large walk-in pantry that was built off the side of the kitchen.

Torie watched him march off appreciatively. "And where is Max? He is my official taster, and I need his help establishing the new menu." She glanced at Fionna, smiling. "Not that I don't appreciate your appreciation, of course, but Max is very discerning, to say the least."

Like Elric, Max was a werewolf as well. He also happened to be the Sheriff of Singing Falls.

"He got a call just as we were leaving the gym to head over," said Elric.

"Tell me why a werewolf, one of the strongest of the supernaturals, needs to work out?" said Jasmin.

"We don't really need to. But it's a way of strengthening our bond. Physical exertion increases our unique pheromone output which in turn——"

Jasmin held up a hand. "So, you get sweaty and smell each other."

Elric shrugged. "Something like that."

Just then his phone pinged, and he slid it out of his pocket, staring at the message. He looked up, eyes hardened.

"Max just texted. He said he needs us to come meet him at the bus station. A body's been found there; one that he says looks like it needs the kind of attention you specialize in."

Hex Education: Chapter Two

Unlike many small towns across the country, there was no "bad side of town" to Singing Falls. The community was uniformly beautiful, with a thriving downtown main street that bisected a set of graded properties to either side, each of those hosting various businesses and shops away from the lively attractions of main street.

The back streets were all lined with evergreens and featured large, central parking lots covered in stone pavers. Around those lots were an array of small townhomes, each with area businesses and mom-and-pop-type stores. There were lawyers' offices adept at setting up financial planning for creatures that lived over two centuries, dry cleaners capable of removing grass, mud and blood stains, shoe repair stores that could custom make coverings for hooved feet, holistic medical clinics that specialized in shifters, and many other services for the community at large.

They were all respectable businesses and would happily take care of any patron that stepped foot on their premises, be they human or other. And while most humans were ignorant of the world around them, they were also happy to be in such a tight-knit community where everyone was welcome, and no one was a stranger.

Unless of course they *were* a stranger, and then they were scrutinized closely by supernatural and human alike. It had taken Torie saving the town from a dark threat on more than one occasion before everyone warmed to her and embraced her as a native.

And that was why Max was so unsettled by the body found behind the bus stop two streets back from main street. Even in broad daylight, no one had seen this young woman get off the bus, walk through the building, or purchase one of the daily Town Crier papers shoved in her backpack. She was propped up against the back of the building next to a door used by one of the two employees who worked for the transit system.

It was one of those employees, Alice Gibbs, who had stumbled upon the girl when she stepped outside to have a smoke. The poor woman had almost tripped over the body, and it appeared to have scared her so badly that she may have just given up smoking altogether, right there on the spot. She was sitting in an old, plastic chair on the opposite side of a dumpster as one of Max's deputies took her statement.

Max was standing next to the body, staring intently, when Torie, Jasmin, Fionna and Elric walked up. Someone had carefully laid a blue vinyl covering over it with the word CORONER written in yellow block print.

Max stood to greet his friends; his typically somber demeanor was even more depressed than usual.

"Max, you said this was something we needed to see,"

Torie said, placing a comforting hand on the big sheriff's shoulder.

He nodded and took a deep breath. "I wasn't sure what to make of this. It's not the typical M.O. for a normal death."

He reached down and drew back the cover, revealing the body of a young girl, probably in her very late teens, maybe twenty, with straight blonde hair that flowed down past her shoulders. She was dressed in jeans that were strategically ripped at the knees and upper thighs, a red tank top, and a blue jean jacket.

The reason for Max's concern was immediately apparent. The girl's eyes were missing. In their place, were blacked-out holes. It looked like she had applied smokey black makeup to the area around where her orbs had once been.

Other than that, there was nothing else to indicate how she might have died.

"No trauma to the body whatsoever," said Max. "No signs of a fight, nothing to indicate what could have done this."

Both Fionna and Elric leaned in closer, noses quivering.

"Yeah, I couldn't detect any scent on her either," Max responded.

"Not only is there no scent of anyone else on her, but *she* doesn't have a scent," said Elric.

"No…there's something there," said Fionna, closing her eyes and inhaling deeper. "It's very faint, but…I can't place it. She smells like old rocks."

"Rocks?" Max said, frowning. "I can't smell that."

"My nose is even more sensitive than a wolf's," she replied. "Most shifters that are prey animals usually are."

Max scribbled in his notebook as Torie and Jasmin leaned in to examine the body.

Jasmin held up both hands, touching the tips of her thumbs and forefingers together to form a triangle, through which she peered.

"Nothing," she said. "There is no magical signature anywhere on the body."

Torie stood, looking around to make sure no one was watching, as her eyes began to glow blue.

> *"I call on spirits to lift any veil,*
> *that may now cause our eyes to fail."*

The whispered incantation caused the body to briefly glow, the faintest of blue light shimmering around the form. It was a brief flash, before dissipating entirely. Torie and Jasmin exchanged looks.

"Nothing," said Torie.

"Those burns around her eyes...what could have done that?" asked Elric. "There is no gun powder or explosive residue. I've never seen anything like this."

"There is also no residual smell in the air of anything inorganic, like wires or plastic burning," said Max.

"So, we can rule out lightning," said Jasmin. "Maybe it was spontaneous human combustion."

Torie's eyes widened. "Are you saying that's real? I was always told that was just something made up by the National Enquirer. You don't know how many sleepless nights I had because of that and quicksand."

Jasmin arched an eyebrow. "For me, it was the Bermuda triangle. I was convinced that at some point in my life I would be flying over it and just disappear."

Max cleared his throat. "It sounds like we are all in

agreement that whatever caused this is not something known to man."

"Or woman," said Fionna, before catching the look everyone gave her. "What? I'm just saying."

"What we know is that this is not a normal death," said Jasmin. "It's definitely supernatural. We just need to figure out what did this."

"Any idea who she was?" asked Torie.

"We're running her face through the missing person's database right now, hoping for a hit," Max replied.

"Any chance she could be a member of the community? Many of the colleges are headed into their breaks next week, maybe she came home a couple days early?" asked Jasmin.

Max shook his head. "It's possible. We are working on that angle as well. But Alice Gibbs knows just about everyone in this town. She's never seen this girl before. And no one inside or outside saw her. We've spoken with the bus driver who pulled in most recently, and he swears she wasn't on the bus."

"So where did she come from?" said Torie, speaking more to herself than the others. "She glanced down at the girl's feet. "Those are Vasque hiking boots she's wearing. They're very well made and not cheap. Waterproof and… great for maintaining your footing around slippery rocks." She glanced at Fionna, nodding.

The squirrel shifter bent close, closing her eyes as she sniffed the boots. Then, she stood, walking around the perimeter of the bus station, staring closely at the ground before moving inside and walking through, doing the same thing.

She came back, shaking her head. "There's nothing. It's almost as if she didn't step foot anywhere near or in the station. Almost as if she was just dropped here out of thin air."

"This has magic written all over it," said Jasmin. "We just need to figure out how."

"And why," added Torie. "I'm assuming she wasn't carrying anything in her bag that stood out; other than that paper, I mean."

Max looked at her, blinking.

"You did check her for ID, didn't you…?" Torie said.

The big werewolf huffed. "I mean, I wasn't the first one on the scene…"

He bent and began rummaging through her bag. Aside from the paper, there were a couple of tubes of lipstick, a hairbrush, compact, bottled water, a couple of health bars, and her wallet. He glanced at Torie, then opened the wallet, searching through it. There was a large amount of cash inside, but no ID of any kind.

"Well, we know that this was deliberate," said Jasmin. "Why else would someone have taken anything to identify her and left all of that money?"

Max unzipped the back pocket of the backpack and reached inside, fishing around. He pulled out a delicate, gold necklace, with a tiny medallion dangling from it.

Jasmin's eyes lit up. "Give that to us. Jewelry can be great transmitters of a person's aura. We might be able to use it to find out more about her."

Torie could see the hesitation on Max's face. This wasn't the first time they had asked him to break the chain of custody, but she also knew he understood the reasoning behind it. While there were a fair number of shifters that made up his force, there were still human political figures he answered to who had no idea how things sometimes had to work in Singing Falls.

He glanced around, then quickly slid the necklace into Jasmin's hand.

"We'll keep this quiet and get it back to you when we can," Torie said. He mumbled in response.

Grab your copy…
vinci-books.com/hexeducation

About the Author

M.J. Caan is an avid reader and writer of all things science fiction and fantasy. Author of multiple science fiction and paranormal fantasy series, M.J. likes to think that there is still magic out there in the world. Even if it's only between the pages of a great book.